Ian McEwan

FIRST LOVE,
LAST RITES

Ian McEwan has written two collections of short
stories—*First Love, Last Rites*, which won the
Somerset Maugham Award, and *In Between the
Sheets*—and five novels: *The Cement Garden; The
Comfort of Strangers*, shortlisted for the 1981 Booker
Prize; *The Child in Time*, winner of the 1987 Whit-
bread Novel of the Year Award; *The Innocent;* and,
most recently, *Black Dogs*, also shortlisted for the
Booker Prize. Mr. McEwan lives in Oxford,
England, with his wife and their four children.

VINTAGE

INTERNATIONAL

BY *Ian McEwan*

NOVELS

The Cement Garden
The Comfort of Strangers
The Child in Time
The Innocent
Black Dogs

STORIES

First Love, Last Rites
In Between the Sheets

PLAYS

The Imitation Game & Other Plays

Ian McEwan

FIRST LOVE, LAST RITES

Vintage International
Vintage Books
A Division of Random House, Inc.
New York

FIRST VINTAGE INTERNATIONAL EDITION, JANUARY 1994

Copyright © 1972, 1973, 1974, 1975 by Ian McEwan

Portions of this book originally appeared in the following
publications: "Disguises" and "Last Day of Summer" in *American
Review;* "Homemade," *New American Review;* "Conversation
with a Cupboard Man," *Transatlantic Review;* "Solid Geometry,"
Amazing Stories.

ISBN: 0-679-75019-3

Author photograph © Jane Bown

Manufactured in the United States of America
10 9 8 7 6 5 4 3 2 1

CONTENTS

Homemade
9

Solid Geometry
31

Last Day of Summer
53

Cocker at the Theatre
73

Butterflies
79

Conversation with a Cupboard Man
97

First Love, Last Rites
115

Disguises
131

To John Webb

Homemade

I can see now our cramped, overlit bathroom and Connie
with a towel draped round her shoulders, sitting on the
edge of the bath weeping, while I filled the sink with warm
water and whistled – such was my elation – 'Teddy Bear'
by Elvis Presley, I can remember, I have always been able
to remember, fluff from the candlewick bedspread swirling
on the surface of the water, but only lately have I fully
realized that if this was the *end* of a particular episode, in so
far as real-life episodes may be said to have an end, it was
Raymond who occupied, so to speak, the beginning and
middle, and if in human affairs there are no such things as
episodes then I should really insist that this story is about
Raymond and not about virginity, coitus, incest and self-
abuse. So let me begin by telling you that it was ironic, for
reasons which will become apparent only very much later
– and you must be patient – it was ironic that Raymond of
all people should want to make me aware of my virginity.
On Finsbury Park one day Raymond approached me, and
steering me across to some laurel bushes bent and unbent
his finger mysteriously before my face and watched me
intently as he did so. I looked on blankly. Then I bent and
unbent my finger too and saw that it was the right thing to
do because Raymond beamed.

'You get it?' he said. 'You get it!' Driven by his

exhilaration I said yes, hoping then that Raymond would leave me alone now to bend and unbend my finger, to come at some understanding of his bewildering digital allegory in solitude. Raymond grasped my lapels with unusual intensity.

'What about it, then?' he gasped. Playing for time, I crooked my forefinger again and slowly straightened it, cool and sure, in fact so cool and sure that Raymond held his breath and stiffened with its motion. I looked at my erect finger and said,

'That depends,' wondering if I was to discover today what it was we were talking of.

Raymond was fifteen then, a year older than I was, and though I counted myself his intellectual superior – which was why I had to pretend to understand the significance of his finger – it was Raymond who *knew* things, it was Raymond who conducted my education. It was Raymond who initiated me into the secrets of adult life which he understood himself intuitively but never totally. The world he showed me, all its fascinating detail, lore and sin, the world for which he was a kind of standing master of ceremonies, never really suited Raymond. He knew that world well enough, but it – so to speak – did not want to know him. So when Raymond produced cigarettes, it was I who learned to inhale the smoke deeply, to blow smoke-rings and to cup my hands round the match like a film star, while Raymond choked and fumbled; and later on when Raymond first got hold of some marihuana, of which I had never heard, it was I who finally got stoned into euphoria while Raymond admitted – something I would never have done myself – that he felt nothing at all. And again, while it was Raymond with his deep voice and wisp of beard who got us into horror films, he would sit through the show with his fingers in his ears and his eyes shut. And that was remarkable in view of the fact that in one month alone we saw twenty-two horror films. When Raymond stole a bottle of whisky from a supermarket in order to introduce me to alcohol, I giggled drunkenly for two hours at Raymond's convulsive fits of vomiting. My first pair of long trousers were a pair belonging to Raymond which he had given to me as a present on my thirteenth birthday. On Raymond they had, like all his clothes, stopped four inches short of his ankles, bulged at the thigh, bagged at the groin and now, as if a parable for our friendship, they fitted me like tailor-mades, in fact so well did they fit me, so comfortable did they feel, that I wore no other trousers for a year. And then there were the thrills of shoplifting. The idea as explained to me by Raymond was quite simple. You walked into Foyle's bookshop, crammed your pockets with books and took them to a dealer on the Mile End Road who was pleased to give you half their cost price. For the very first occasion I borrowed my father's overcoat which trailed the pavement magnificently as I swept along. I met Raymond outside the shop. He was in shirtsleeves because he had left his coat on the Underground but he was certain he could manage without one anyway, so we went into the shop. While I stuffed into my many pockets a selection of slim volumes of prestigious verse, Raymond was concealing on his person the seven volumes of the Variorum Edition of the Works of Edmund Spenser. For anyone else the boldness of the act might have offered some chance of success, but Raymond's boldness had a precarious quality, closer in fact to a complete detachment from the realities of the situation. The under-manager stood behind Raymond as he plucked the books from the shelf. The two of them were standing by the door as I brushed by with my own load, and I gave Raymond, who still clasped the tomes about him, a conspiratorial smile, and thanked the under-manager who automatically held the door open for me. Fortunately, so hopeless was Raymond's attempt at shoplifting, so idiotic and transparent his excuses, that the manager finally let him go, liberally assuming him to be, I suppose, mentally deranged.

And finally, and perhaps most significantly, Raymond acquainted me with the dubious pleasures of masturbation. At the time I was twelve, the dawn of my sexual day. We were exploring a cellar on a bomb site, poking around to see what the dossers had left behind, when Raymond, having lowered his trousers as if to have a piss, began to rub his prick with a coruscating vigour, inviting me to do the same. I did and soon became suffused with a warm, indistinct pleasure which intensified to a floating, melting sensation as if my guts might at any time drift away to nothing. And all this time our hands pumped furiously. I was beginning to congratulate Raymond on his discovery of such a simple, inexpensive yet pleasurable way of passing the time, and at the same time wondering if I could not dedicate my whole life to this glorious sensation – and I suppose looking back now in many respects I have – I was about to express all manner of things when I was lifted by the scruff of the neck, my arms, my legs, my insides, haled, twisted, racked, and producing for all this two dollops of sperm which flipped over Raymond's Sunday jacket – it was Sunday – and dribbled into his breast pocket.

'Hey,' he said, breaking with his action, 'what did you do that for?' Still recovering from this devastating experience I said nothing, I could not say anything.

'I show you how to do this,' harangued Raymond, dabbing delicately at the glistening jissom on his dark jacket, 'and all you can do is spit.'

And so by the age of fourteen I had acquired, with

Raymond's guidance, a variety of pleasures which I
rightly associated with the adult world. I smoked about
ten cigarettes a day, I drank whisky when it was available,
I had a connoisseur's taste for violence and obscenity, I
had smoked the heady resin of *cannabis sativa* and I was
aware of my own sexual precocity, though oddly it never
occurred to me to find any use for it, my imagination as
yet unnourished by longings or private fantasies. And all
these pastimes were financed by the dealer in the Mile End
Road. For these acquired tastes Raymond was my
Mephistopheles, he was a clumsy Virgil to my Dante,
showing me the way to a Paradiso where he himself could
not tread. He could not smoke because it made him cough,
the whisky made him ill, the films frightened or bored him,
the cannabis did not affect him, and while I made stalac-
tites on the ceiling of the bomb-site cellar, he made nothing
at all.

'Perhaps,' he said mournfully as we were leaving the
site one afternoon, 'perhaps I'm a little too old for that
sort of thing.'

So when Raymond stood before me now intently
crooking and straightening his finger I sensed that here
was yet another fur-lined chamber of that vast, gloomy
and delectable mansion, adulthood, and that if I only held
back a little, concealing, for pride's sake, my ignorance,
then shortly Raymond would reveal and then shortly I
would excel.

'Well, that depends.' We walked across Finsbury Park
where once Raymond, in his earlier, delinquent days had
fed glass splinters to the pigeons, where together, in innocent bliss worthy of the 'Prelude', we had roasted alive
Sheila Harcourt's budgerigar while she swooned on the
grass nearby, where as young boys we had crept behind
bushes to hurl rocks at the couples fucking in the arbour;

across Finsbury Park then, and Raymond saying,

'Who do you know?' Who did I know? I was still blundering, and this could be a change of subject, for Raymond had an imprecise mind. So I said, 'Who do *you* know?' to which Raymond replied, 'Lulu Smith,' and made everything clear – or at least the subject matter, for my innocence was remarkable. Lulu Smith! Dinky Lulu! the very name curls a chilly hand round my balls. Lulu Lamour, of whom it was said she would do anything, and that she had done everything. There were Jewish jokes, elephant jokes and there were Lulu jokes, and these were mainly responsible for the extravagant legend. Lulu Slim – but how my mind reels – whose physical enormity was matched only by the enormity of her reputed sexual appetite and prowess, her grossness only by the grossness she inspired, the legend only by the reality. Zulu Lulu! who – so fame had it – had laid a trail across north London of frothing idiots, a desolation row of broken minds and pricks spanning Shepherds Bush to Holloway, Ongar to Islington. Lulu! Her wobbling girth and laughing piggy's eyes, blooming thighs and dimpled finger-joints, this heaving, steaming leg-load of schoolgirl flesh who had, so reputation insisted, had it with a giraffe, a humming-bird, a man in an iron lung (who had subsequently died), a yak, Cassius Clay, a marmoset, a Mars Bar and the gear stick of her grandfather's Morris Minor (and subsequently a traffic warden).

Finsbury Park was filled with the spirit of Lulu Smith and I felt for the first time ill-defined longings as well as mere curiosity. I knew approximately what was to be done, for had I not seen heaped couples in all corners of the park during the long summer evenings, and had I not thrown stones and water bombs? – something I now superstitiously regretted. And suddenly there in Finsbury

Park, as we threaded our way through the pert piles of dog shit, I was made aware of and resented my virginity; I knew it to be the last room in the mansion, I knew it to be for certain the most luxurious, its furnishings more elaborate than any other room, its attractions more deadly, and the fact that I had never had it, made it, done it, was a total anathema, my malodorous albatross, and I looked to Raymond, who still held his forefinger stiff before him, to reveal what I must do. Raymond was bound to know ...

After school Raymond and I went to a cafe near Finsbury Park Odeon. While others of our age picked their noses over their stamp collections or homework, Raymond and I spent many hours here, discussing mostly easy ways of making money, and drinking large mugs of tea. Sometimes we got talking to the workmen who came there. Millais should have been there to paint us as we listened transfixed to their unintelligible fantasies and exploits, of deals with lorry drivers, lead from church roofs, fuel missing from the City Engineer's department, and then of cunts, bits, skirt, of strokings, beatings, fuckings, suckings, of arses and tits, behind, above, below, in front, with, without, of scratching and tearing, licking and shitting, of juiced cunts streaming, warm and infinite, of others cold and arid but worth a try, of pricks old and limp, or young and ebullient, of coming, too soon, too late or not at all, of how many times a day, of attendant diseases, of pus and swellings, cankers and regrets, of poisoned ovaries and destitute testicles; we listened to who and how the dustmen fucked, how the Co-op milkmen fitted it in, what the coalmen could hump, what the carpet-fitter could lay, what the builders could erect, what the meter man could inspect, what the bread man could deliver, the gas man sniff out, the plumber plumb, the electrician connect, the doctor inject, the lawyer solicit, the furniture man install –

and so on, in an unreal complex of timeworn puns and innuendo, formulas, slogans, folklore and bravado. I listened without understanding, remembering and filing away anecdotes which I would one day use myself, putting by histories of perversions and sexual manners – in fact a whole sexual morality, so that when finally I began to understand, from my own experience, what it was all about, I had on tap a complete education which, augmented by a quick reading of the more interesting parts of Havelock Ellis and Henry Miller, earned me the reputation of being the juvenile connoisseur of coitus to whom dozens of males – and fortunately females, too – came to seek advice. And all this, a reputation which followed me into art college and enlivened my career there, all this after only one fuck – the subject of this story.

So it was there in the cafe where I had listened, remembered and understood nothing that Raymond now relaxed his forefinger at last to curl it round the handle of his cup, and said,

'Lulu Smith will let you see it for a shilling.' I was glad of that. I was glad we were not rushing into things, glad that I would not be left alone with Zulu Lulu and be expected to perform the terrifyingly obscure, glad that the first encounter of this necessary adventure would be reconnaissance. And besides, I had only ever seen two naked females in my life. The obscene films we patronized in those days were nowhere near obscene enough, showing only the legs, backs and ecstatic faces of happy couples, leaving the rest to our tumescent imaginations, and clarifying nothing. As for the two naked women, my mother was vast and grotesque, the skin hanging from her like flayed toad-hides, and my ten-year-old sister was an ugly bat whom as a child I could hardly bring myself to look at, let along share the bath-tub with. And after all, a shilling was no expense at all, considering that Raymond and I were richer than most of the workmen in the cafe. In fact I was richer than any of my many uncles or my poor overworked father or anyone else I knew in my family. I used to laugh when I thought of the twelve-hour shift my father worked in the flour mill, of his exhausted, blanched, ill-tempered face when he got home in the evening, and I laughed a little louder when I thought of the thousands who each morning poured out of the terraced houses like our own to labour through the week, rest up on Sunday and then back again on Monday to toil in the mills, factories, timber yards and quaysides of London, returning each night older, more tired and no richer; over our cups of tea I laughed with Raymond at this quiescent betrayal of a lifetime, heaving, digging, shoving, packing, checking, sweating and groaning for the profits of others, at how, to reassure themselves, they made a virtue of this lifetime's grovel, at how they prized themselves for never missing a day in the inferno; and most of all I laughed when uncles Bob or Ted or my father made me a present of one of their hard-earned shillings – and on special occasions a ten-shilling note – I laughed because I knew that a good afternoon's work in the bookshop earned more than they scraped together in a week. I had to laugh discreetly, of course, for it would not do to mess up a gift like that, especially when it was quite obvious that they derived a great deal of pleasure from giving it to me. I can see them now, one of my uncles or my father striding the tiny length of the front parlour, the coin or banknote in his hand, reminiscing, anecdoting and advising me on Life, poised before the luxury of giving, and feeling good, feeling so good that it was a joy to watch. They felt, and for that short period they were, grand, wise, reflective, kind-hearted and expansive, and perhaps, who knows, a little divine; patricians dispensing to their son or nephew in the wisest, most generous way, the fruits of their sagacity and wealth – they were gods in their own temple and who was I to refuse their gift? Kicked in the arse round the factory fifty hours a week they needed these parlour miracle-plays, these mythic confrontations between Father and Son, so I, being appreciative and sensible of all the nuances of the situation, accepted their money, at the risk of boredom played along a little and suppressed my amusement till afterwards when I was made weak with tearful, hooting laughter. Long before I knew it I was a student, a promising student, of irony.

A shilling then was not too much to pay for a glimpse at the incommunicable, the heart of mystery's mystery, the Fleshly Grail, Dinky Lulu's pussy, and I urged Raymond to arrange a viewing as soon as possible. Raymond was already sliding into his role of stage manager, furrowing his brow in an important way, humming about dates, times, places, payments, and drawing ciphers on the back of an envelope. Raymond was one of those rare people who not only derive great pleasure from organizing events, but also are forlornly bad at doing it. It was quite possible that we would arrive on the wrong day at the wrong time, that there would be confusion about payment or the length of viewing time, but there was one thing which was ultimately more certain than anything else, more certain than the sun rising tomorrow, and that was that we would finally be shown the exquisite quim. For life was undeniably on Raymond's side; while in those days I could not have put my feelings into so many words, I sensed that in the cosmic array of individual fates Raymond's was cast diametrically opposite mine. Fortuna played practical jokes on Raymond, perhaps she even kicked sand in his eyes, but she never spat in his face or trod deliberately on

his existential corns – Raymond's mistakings, losses, be-
trayals and injuries were all, in the final estimate, comic
rather than tragic. I remember one occasion when
Raymond paid seventeen pounds for a two-ounce cake of
hashish which turned out not to be hashish at all. To cover
his losses Raymond took the lump to a well-known spot in
Soho and tried to sell it to a plainclothes man who
fortunately did not press a charge. After all, there was, at
that time at least, no law against dealing in powdered
horse-dung, even if it was wrapped in tinfoil. Then there
was the cross-country. Raymond was a mediocre runner
and was among ten others chosen to represent the school
in the sub-counties meeting. I always went along to the
meetings. In fact there was no other sport I watched with
such good heart, such entertainment and elation as a good
cross-country. I loved the racked, contorted faces of the
runners as they came up the tunnel of flags and crossed the
finishing line; I found especially interesting those who
came after the first fifty or so, running harder than any of
the other contestants and competing demoniacally among
themselves for the hundred and thirteenth place in the field.
I watched them stumble up the tunnel of flags, clawing at
their throats, retching, flailing their arms and falling to
the grass, convinced that I had before me here a vision of
human futility. Only the first thirty runners counted for
anything in the contest and once the last of these had
arrived the group of spectators began to disperse, leaving
the rest to fight their private battles – and it was at this
point that my interest pricked up. Long after the judges,
marshals and time-keepers had gone home I remained at
the finishing line in the descending gloom of a late winter's
afternoon to watch the last of the runners crawl across the
end marker. Those who fell I helped to their feet, I gave
handkerchiefs to bloody noses, I thumped vomiters on the

back, I massaged cramped calves and toes – a real
Florence Nightingale, in fact, with the difference that I felt
an elation, a gay fascination with the triumphant spirit of
human losers who had run themselves into the ground for
nothing at all. How my mind soared, how my eyes swam,
when, after having waited ten, fifteen, even twenty minutes
in that vast, dismal field, surrounded on all sides by
factories, pylons, dull houses and garages, a cold wind
rising, bringing the beginnings of a bitter drizzle, waiting
there in that heavy gloom – and then suddenly to discern
on the far side of the field a limp white blob slowly making
its way to the tunnel, slowly measuring out with numb feet
on the wet grass its micro-destiny of utter futility. And
there beneath the brooding metropolitan sky, as if to unify
the complex totality of organic evolution and human purpose and place it within my grasp, the tiny amoebic blob
across the field took on human shape and yet still it held to
the same purpose, staggering determinedly in its pointless
effort to reach the flags – just life, just faceless, self-
renewing life to which, as the figure jack knifed to the
ground by the finishing line, my heart warmed, my spirit
rose in the fulsome abandonment of morbid and fatal
identification with the cosmic life process – the Logos.

'Bad luck, Raymond,' I would say cheerily as I handed
him his sweater, 'better luck next time.' And smiling wanly
with the sure, sad knowledge of Arlecchino, of Feste, the
knowledge that of the two it is the Comedian, not the
Tragedian, who holds the Trump, the twenty-second
Arcanum, whose letter is Than, whose symbol is Sol,
smiling as we left the now almost dark field, Raymond
would say,

'Well, it was only a cross-country, only a game, you
know.'

Raymond promised to confront the divine Lulu Smith

with our proposition the following day after school, and since I was pledged to look after my sister that evening while my parents were at the Walthamstow dog track, I said goodbye to Raymond there at the cafe. All the way home I thought about cunt. I saw it in the smile of the conductress, I heard it in the roar of the traffic, I smelt it in the fumes from the shoe-polish factory, conjectured it beneath the skirts of passing housewives, felt it at my finger tips, sensed it in the air, drew it in my mind and at supper, which was toad-in-the-hole, I devoured, as in an unspeakable rite, genitalia of batter and sausage. And for all this I still did not know just exactly what a cunt was. I eyed my sister across the table. I exaggerated a little just now when I said she was an ugly bat – I was beginning to think that perhaps she was not so bad-looking after all. Her teeth protruded, that could not be denied, and if her cheeks were a little too sunken it was not so you would notice in the dark, and when her hair had been washed, as it was now, you could almost pass her off as plain. So it was not surprising that I came to be thinking over my toad-in-the-hole that with some cajoling and perhaps a little honest deceit Connie could be persuaded to think of herself, if only for a few minutes, as something more than a sister, as, let us say, a beautiful young lady, a film star and maybe, Connie, we could slip into bed here and try out this rather moving scene, now you get out of these clumsy pyjamas while I see to the light ... And armed with this comfortably gained knowledge I could face the awesome Lulu with zeal and abandon, the whole terrifying ordeal would pale into insignificance, and who knows, perhaps I could lay her out there and then, halfway through the peepshow.

I never enjoyed looking after Connie. She was petulant, demanding, spoiled and wanted to play games all the while instead of watching the television. I usually managed to get her to bed an hour early by winding the clock forward. Tonight I wound it back. As soon as my mother and father had left for the dog track I asked Connie which games she would like to play, she could choose anything she liked.

'I don't want to play games with you.'

'Why not?'

'Because you were staring at me all the time through supper.'

'Well, of course I was, Connie. I was trying to think of the games you liked to play best and I was just looking at you, that was all.' Finally she agreed to play hide and seek, which I had suggested with special insistence because our house was of such a size that there were only two rooms you could hide in, and they were both bedrooms. Connie was to hide first. I covered my eyes and counted to thirty, listening all the while to her footsteps in my parents' bedroom directly above, hearing with satisfaction the creak of the bed – she was hiding under the eiderdown, her second favourite place. I shouted 'Coming' and began to mount the stairs. At the bottom of the stairs I do not think I had decided clearly what I was about to do; perhaps just look around, see where things were, draw a mental plan for future reference – after all it would not do to go scaring my little sister who would not think twice about telling my father everything, and that would mean a scene of some sort, laborious lies to invent, shouting and crying and that sort of thing, just at a time when I needed all my energy for the obsession in hand. By the time I reached the top of the stairs, however, the blood having drained from brain to groin, literally, one might say, from sense to sensibility, by the time I was catching my breath on the top stair and closing my moist hand round the bedroom door-handle, I had decided to rape my sister. Gently I pushed the door open and called in a sing-song voice,

'Connieee, where aaare you?' That usually made her giggle, but this time there was no sound. Holding my breath I tip-toed over to the bedside and sang,

'I knooow where youuu are,' and bending down by the tell-tale lump under the eiderdown, I whispered,

'I'm coming to get you,' and began to peel the bulky cover away, softly, almost tenderly, peeking into the dark warmth underneath. Dizzy with expectation I drew it right back, and there, helplessly and innocently stretched out before me were my parents' pyjamas, and even as I was leaping back in surprise I received a blow in the small of my back of such unthinking vigour as can only be inflicted by a sister on her brother. And there was Connie dancing with mirth, the wardrobe door swinging open behind her.

'I saw you, I saw you and you didn't see me!' To relieve my feelings I kicked her shins and sat on the bed to consider what next, while Connie, predictably histrionic, sat on the floor and boo-hooed. I found the noise depressing after a while so I went downstairs and read the paper, certain that soon Connie would follow me down. She did, and she was sulking.

'What game do you want to play now?' I asked her. She sat on the edge of the sofa pouting and sniffing and hating me. I was even considering forgetting the whole plan and giving myself up to an evening's television when I had an idea, an idea of such simplicity, elegance, clarity and formal beauty, an idea which wore the assurance of its own success like a tailor-made suit. There is a game which all home-loving, unimaginative little girls like Connie find irresistible, a game which, ever since she had learned to speak the necessary words, Connie had plagued me to play with her, so that my boyhood years were haunted by her pleadings and exorcised by my inevitable refusals; it was a game, in short, which I would rather be burned at the stake for than have my friends see me play it. And now at last we were going to play Mummies and Daddies.

'*I* know a game you'd like to play, Connie,' I said. Of course she would not reply, but I let my words hang there in the air like bait. 'I know a game *you'd* like to play.' She lifted her head.

'What is it?'

'It's a game you're always wanting to play.'

She brightened. 'Mummies and Daddies?' She was transformed, she was ecstatic. She fetched prams, dolls, stoves, fridges, cots, teacups, a washing machine and a kennel from her room and set them up around me in a flutter of organizational zeal.

'Now you go here, no there, and this can be the kitchen and this is the door where you come in and don't tread on there because there's a wall and I come in and see you and I say to you and then you say to me and you go out and I make lunch.' I was plunged into the microcosm of the dreary, everyday, ponderous banalities, the horrifying, niggling details of the life of our parents and their friends, the life that Connie so dearly wanted to ape. I went to work and came back, I went to the pub and came back, I posted a letter and came back, I went to the shops and came back, I read a paper, I pinched the Bakelite cheeks of my progeny, I read another paper, pinched some more cheeks, went to work and came back. And Connie? She just cooked on the stove, washed up in the sink unit, washed, fed, put to sleep and roused her sixteen dolls and then poured some more tea – and she was happy. She was the inter-galactic-earth-goddess-housewife, she owned and

controlled all around her, she saw all, she knew all, she
told me when to go out, when to come in, which room I
was in, what to say, how and when to say it. She was
happy. She was complete, I have never seen another
human so complete, she smiled, wide open, joyous and
innocent smiles which I have never seen since – she tasted
paradise on earth. And one point she was so blocked with
the wonder, the ecstasy of it all, that mid-sentence her
words choked up and she sat back on her heels, her eyes
glistening, and breathed one long musical sigh of rare and
wonderful happiness. It was almost a shame I had it in
mind to rape her. Returning from work the twentieth time
that half hour I said,

'Connie, we're leaving out one of the most important
things that Mummies and Daddies do together.' She could
hardly believe we had left anything out and she was
curious to know.

'They fuck together, Connie, surely you know about
that.'

'Fuck?' On her lips the word sounded strangely mean-
ingless, which in a way I suppose it was, as far as I was
concerned. The whole idea was to give it some meaning.

'Fuck? What does that mean?'

'Well, it's what they do at night, when they go to bed at
night, just before they go to sleep.'

'Show me.' I explained that we would have to go upstairs and get into bed.

'No, we don't. We can pretend and this can be the bed,'
she said, pointing at a square made by the design of the
carpet.

'I cannot pretend and show it to you at the same time.'
So once again I was climbing the stairs, once again my
blood pounding and my manhood proudly stirring.
Connie was quite excited too, still delirious with the

happiness of the game and pleased at the novel turn it was taking.

'The first thing they do', I said, as I led her to the bed, 'is to take off all their clothes.' I pushed her on to the bed and, with fingers almost useless with agitation, unbuttoned her pyjamas till she sat naked before me, still sweet-smelling from her bath and giggling with the fun of it all. Then I got undressed too, leaving my pants on so as not to alarm her, and sat by her side. As children we had seen enough of each other's bodies to take our nakedness for granted, though that was some time ago now and I sensed her unease.

'Are you sure this is what they do?'

My own uncertainty was obscured now by lust. 'Yes,' I said, 'it's quite simple. You have a hole there and I put my weenie in it.' She clasped her hand over her mouth, giggling incredulously.

'That's silly. Why do they want to do that?' I had to admit it to myself, there was something unreal about it.

'They do it because it's their way of saying they like each other.' Connie was beginning to think that I was making the whole thing up, which, again, in a way I suppose I was. She stared at me, wide-eyed.

'But that's daft, why don't they just tell each other?' I was on the defensive, a mad scientist explaining his new crack-pot invention – coitus – before an audience of sceptical rationalists.

'Look,' I said to my sister, 'it's not only that. It's also a very nice feeling. They do it to get that feeling.'

'To get the feeling?' She still did not quite believe me. 'Get the feeling? What do you mean, get the feeling?'

I said, 'I'll show you.' And at the same time I pushed Connie on to the bed and lay on top of her in the manner I

had inferred from the films Raymond and I had seen together. I was still wearing my underpants. Connie stared
blankly up at me, not even afraid – in fact, she might have
been closer to boredom. I writhed from side to side, trying
to push my pants off without getting up.

'I still don't get it,' she complained from underneath me.
'I'm not getting any feeling. Are you getting any feeling?'

'Wait,' I grunted, as I hooked the underpants round the
end of my toes with the very tips of my fingers, 'if you just
wait a minute I'll show you.' I was beginning to lose my
temper with Connie, with myself, with the universe, but
mostly with my underpants which snaked determinedly
round my ankles. At last I was free. My prick was
hard and sticky on Connie's belly and now I began to
manœuvre it between her legs with one hand while I
supported the weight of my body with the other. I searched
her tiny crevice without the least notion of what I was
looking for, but half expecting all the same to be transformed at any moment into a human whirlwind of sensation. I think perhaps I had in mind a warm fleshy
chamber, but as I prodded and foraged, jabbed and
wheedled, I found nothing other than tight, resisting skin.
Meanwhile Connie just lay on her back, occasionally
making little comments.

'Ooh, that's where I go wee-wee. I'm sure *our* mummy
and daddy don't do this.' My supporting arm was being
seared by pins and needles, I was feeling raw and yet still
I poked and pushed, in a mood of growing despair. Each
time Connie said, 'I still don't get any feeling,' I felt
another ounce of my manhood slip away. Finally I had to
rest. I sat on the edge of the bed to consider my hopeless
failure, while behind me Connie propped herself up on her
elbows. After a moment or two I felt the bed begin to
shake with silent spasms and, turning, I saw Connie with

tears spilling down her screwed-up face, inarticulate and writhing with choked laughter.

'What is it?' I asked, but she could only point vaguely in my direction and groan, and then she lay back on the bed, heaving and helpless with mirth. I sat by her side, not knowing what to think but deciding, as Connie quaked behind me, that another attempt was now out of the question. At last she was able to get out some words. She sat up and pointed at my still erect prick and gasped,

'It looks so ... it looks so ...' sank back in another fit, and then managed in one squeal, '*So silly, it looks so silly,*' after which she collapsed again into a high-pitched, squeezed-out titter. I sat there in lonely detumescent blankness, numbed by this final humiliation into the realization that this was no real girl beside me, this was no true representative of that sex; this was no boy, certainly, nor was it finally a girl – it was my sister, after all. I stared down at my limp prick, wondering at its hang-dog look, and just as I was thinking of getting my clothes together, Connie, silent now, touched me on the elbow.

'I know where it goes,' she said, and lay back on the bed, her legs wide apart, something it had not occurred to me to ask her to do. She settled herself among the pillows. 'I know where the hole is.'

I forgot my sister and my prick rose inquisitively, hope-fully, to the invitation which Connie was whispering. It was all right with her now, she was at Mummies and Daddies and controlling the game again. With her hand she guided me into her tight, dry little-girl's cunt and we lay perfectly still for a while. I wished Raymond could have seen me, and I was glad he had brought my virginity to my notice, I wished Dinky Lulu could have seen me, in fact if my wishes had been granted I would have had all my friends, all the people I knew, file through the bedroom to catch me in my splendorous pose. For more than sensation, more than any explosion behind my eyes, spears through my stomach, searings in my groin or rackings of my soul – more than any of these things, none of which I felt anyway, more then than even the thought of these things, I felt proud, proud to be fucking, even if it were only Connie, my ten-year-old sister, even if it had been a crippled mountain goat I would have been proud to be lying there in that manly position, proud in advance of being able to say 'I have fucked', of belonging intimately and irrevocably to that superior half of humanity who had known coitus, and fertilized the world with it. Connie lay quite still too, her eyes half-closed, breathing deeply – she was asleep. It was way past her bedtime and our strange game had exhausted her. For the first time I moved gently backwards and forwards, just a few times, and came in a miserable, played-out, barely pleasurable way. It woke Connie into indignation.

'You've wet inside me,' and she began to cry. Hardly noticing, I got up and started to get dressed. This may have been one of the most desolate couplings known to copulating mankind, involving lies, deceit, humiliation, incest, my partner falling asleep, my gnat's orgasm and the sobbing which now filled the bedroom, but I was pleased with it, myself, Connie, pleased to let things rest a while, to let the matter drop. I led Connie to the bathroom and began to fill the sink – my parents would be back soon and Connie should be asleep in her bed. I had made it into the adult world finally, I was pleased about that, but right then I did not want to see a naked girl, or a naked anything for a while yet. Tomorrow I would tell Raymond to forget the appointment with Lulu, unless he wanted to go it alone. And I knew for a fact that he would not want that at all.

Solid Geometry

In Melton Mowbray in 1875 at an auction of articles of 'curiosity and worth', my great-grandfather, in the company of M his friend, bid for the penis of Captain Nicholls who died in Horsemonger jail in 1873. It was bottled in a glass twelve inches long, and, noted my great-grandfather in his diary that night, 'in a beautiful state of preservation'. Also for auction was 'the unnamed portion of the late Lady Barrymore. It went to Sam Israels for fifty guineas.' My great-grandfather was keen on the idea of having the two items as a pair, and M dissuaded him. This illustrates perfectly their friendship. My great-grandfather the excitable theorist, M the man of action who knew when to bid at auctions. My great-grandfather lived for sixty-nine years. For forty-five of them, at the end of every day, he sat down before going to bed and wrote his thoughts in a diary. These diaries are on my table now, forty-five volumes bound in calf leather, and to the left sits Capt. Nicholls in the glass jar. My great-grandfather lived on the income derived from the patent of an invention of his father, a handy fastener used by corset-makers right up till the outbreak of the First World War. My great-grandfather liked gossip, numbers and theories. He also liked tobacco, good port, jugged hare and, very occasionally, opium. He liked to think of himself as a mathematician, though he never had a job, and never published a book. Nor did he ever travel or get his name in *The Times*, even when he died. In 1869 he married Alice, only daughter of the Rev. Toby Shadwell, co-author of a not highly regarded book on English wild flowers. I believe my great-grandfather to have been a very fine diarist, and when I have finished editing the diaries and they are published I am certain he will receive the recognition due to him. When my work is over I will take a long holiday, travel somewhere cold and clean and treeless, Iceland or the Russian Steppes. I used to think that at the end of it all I would try, if it was possible, to divorce my wife Maisie, but now there is no need at all.

Often Maisie would shout in her sleep and I would have to wake her.

'Put your arm around me,' she would say. 'It was a horrible dream. I had it once before. I was in a plane flying over a desert. But it wasn't really a desert. I took the plane lower and I could see there were thousands of babies heaped up, stretching away into the horizon, all of them naked and climbing over each other. I was running out of fuel and I had to land the plane. I tried to find a space, I flew on and on looking for a space...'

'Go to sleep now,' I said through a yawn. 'It was only a dream.'

'No,' she cried. 'I mustn't go to sleep, not just yet.'

'Well, *I* have to sleep now,' I told her. 'I have to be up early in the morning.'

She shook my shoulder. 'Please don't go to sleep yet, don't leave me here.'

'I'm in the same bed,' I said. 'I won't leave you.'

'It makes no difference, don't leave me awake ...' But my eyes were already closing.

Lately I have taken up my great-grandfather's habit.

Before going to bed I sit down for half an hour and think over the day. I have no mathematical whimsies or sexual theories to note down. Mostly I write out what Maisie has said to me and what I have said to Maisie. Sometimes, for complete privacy, I lock myself in the bathroom, sit on the toilet seat and balance the writing-pad on my knees. Apart from me there is occasionally a spider or two in the bathroom. They climb up the waste pipe and crouch perfectly still on the glaring white enamel. They must wonder where they have come to. After hours of crouching they turn back, puzzled, or perhaps disappointed they could not learn more. As far as I can tell, my great-grandfather made only one reference to spiders. On May 8th, 1906, he wrote, 'Bismarck is a spider.'

In the afternoons Maisie used to bring me tea and tell me her nightmares. Usually I was going through old newspapers, compiling indexes, cataloguing items, putting down this volume, picking up another. Maisie said she was in a bad way. Recently she had been sitting around the house all day glancing at books on psychology and the occult, and almost every night she had bad dreams. Since the time we exchanged physical blows, lying in wait to hit each other with the same shoe outside the bathroom, I had had little sympathy for her. Part of her problem was jealousy. She was very jealous ... of my great-grandfather's forty-five-volume diary, and of my purpose and energy in editing it. She was doing nothing. I was putting down one volume and picking up another when Maisie came in with the tea.

'Can I tell you my dream?' she asked. 'I was flying this plane over a kind of desert ...'

'Tell me later, Maisie,' I said. 'I'm in the middle of something here.' After she had gone I stared at the wall in front of my desk and thought about M, who came to talk and dine with my great-grandfather regularly over a period of fifteen years up until his sudden and unexplained departure one evening in 1898. M, whoever he might have been, was something of an academic, as well as a man of action. For example, on the evening of August 9th, 1870, the two of them are talking about positions for lovemaking and M tells my great-grandfather that copulation *a posteriori* is the most natural way owing to the position of the clitoris and because other anthropoids favour this method. My great-grandfather, who copulated about half-a-dozen times in his entire life, and that with Alice during the first year of their marriage, wondered out loud what the Church's view was and straight away M is able to tell him that the seventh-century theologian Theodore considered copulation *a posteriori* a sin ranking with masturbation and therefore worthy of forty penances. Later in the same evening my great-grandfather produced mathematical evidence that the maximum number of positions cannot exceed the prime number seventeen. M scoffed at this and told him he had seen a collection of drawings by Romano, a pupil of Raphael's, in which twenty-four positions were shown. And, he said, he had heard of a Mr F. K. Forberg who had accounted for ninety. By the time I remembered the tea Maisie had left by my elbow it was cold.

An important stage in the deterioration of our marriage was reached as follows. I was sitting in the bathroom one evening writing out a conversation Maisie and I had had about the Tarot pack when suddenly she was outside, rapping on the door and rattling the door-handle.

'Open the door,' she called out. 'I want to come in.'

I said to her, 'You'll have to wait a few minutes more. I've almost finished.'

'Let me in now,' she shouted. 'You're not using the toilet.'

'Wait,' I replied, and wrote another line or two. Now Maisie was kicking the door.

'My period has started and I need to get something.' I ignored her yells and finished my piece, which I considered to be particularly important. If I left it till later certain details would be lost. There was no sound from Maisie now and I assumed she was in the bedroom. But when I opened the door she was standing right in my way with a shoe in her hand. She brought the heel of it sharply down on my head, and I only had time to move slightly to one side. The heel caught the top of my ear and cut it badly.

'There,' said Maisie, stepping round me to get to the bathroom, 'now we are both bleeding,' and she banged the door shut. I picked up the shoe and stood quietly and patiently outside the bathroom holding a handkerchief to my bleeding ear. Maisie was in the bathroom about ten minutes and as she came out I caught her neatly and squarely on the top of her head. I did not give her time to move. She stood perfectly still for a moment looking straight into my eyes.

'You worm,' she breathed, and went down to the kitchen to nurse her head out of my sight.

During supper yesterday Maisie claimed that a man locked in a cell with only the Tarot cards would have access to all knowledge. She had been doing a reading that afternoon and the cards were still spread about the floor.

'Could he work out the street plan of Valparaiso from the cards?' I asked.

'You're being stupid,' she replied.

'Could it tell him the best way to start a laundry business, the best way to make an omelette or a kidney machine?'

'Your mind is so narrow,' she complained. 'You're so narrow, so predictable.'

'Could he', I insisted, 'tell me who M is, or why ...'

'Those things don't matter,' she cried. 'They're not necessary.'

'They are still knowledge. Could he find them out?'

She hesitated. 'Yes, he could.'

I smiled, and said nothing.

'What's so funny?' she said. I shrugged, and she began to get angry. She wanted to be disproved. 'Why did you ask all those pointless questions?'

I shrugged again. 'I just wanted to know if you really meant *everything*.'

Maisie banged the table and screamed, 'Damn you! Why are you always trying me out? Why don't you say something real?' And with that we both recognized we had reached the point where all our discussions led and we became bitterly silent.

Work on the diaries cannot proceed until I have cleared up the mystery surrounding M. After coming to dinner on and off for fifteen years and supplying my great-grand-father with a mass of material for his theories, M simply disappears from the pages of the diary. On Tuesday, December 6th, my great-grandfather invited M to dine on the following Saturday, and although M came, my great-grandfather in the entry for that day simply writes, 'M to dinner.' On any other day the conversation at these meals is recorded at great length. M had been to dinner on Monday, December 5th, and the conversation had been about geometry, and the entries for the rest of that week are entirely given over to the same subject. There is absolutely no hint of antagonism. Besides, my great-grandfather *needed* M. M provided his material, M knew what was going on, he was familiar with London and he had been on the Continent a number of times. He knew all about socialism and Darwin, he had an acquaintance in the free love movement, a friend of James Hinton. M was *in* the world in a way which my great-grandfather, who left Melton Mowbray only once in his lifetime, to visit Nottingham, was not. Even as a young man my great-grandfather preferred to theorize by the fireside; all he needed were the materials M supplied. For example, one evening in June 1884 M, who was just back from London, gave my great-grandfather an account of how the streets of the town were fouled and clogged by horse dung. Now in that same week my great-grandfather had been reading the essay by Malthus called 'On the Principle of Population'. That night he made an excited entry in the diary about a pamphlet he wanted to write and have published. It was to be called 'De Stercore Equorum'. The pamphlet was never published and probably never written, but there are detailed notes in the diary entries for the two weeks following that evening. In 'De Stercore Equorum' ('Concerning Horseshit') he assumes geometric growth in the horse population, and working from detailed street plans he predicted that the metropolis would be impassable by 1935. By impassable he took to mean an average thickness of one foot (compressed) in every major street. He described involved experiments outside his own stables to determine the compressibility of horse dung, which he managed to express mathematically. It was all pure theory, of course. His results rested on the assumption that no dung would be shovelled aside in the fifty years to come. Very likely it was M who talked my great-grandfather out of the project.

One morning, after a long dark night of Maisie's nightmares, we were lying side by side in bed and I said,

'What is it you really want? Why don't you go back to your job? These long walks, all this analysis, sitting around the house, lying in bed all morning, the Tarot pack, the nightmares ... what is it you want?'

And she said, 'I want to get my head straight,' which she had said many times before.

I said, 'Your head, your mind, it's not like a hotel kitchen, you know, you can't throw stuff out like old tin cans. It's more like a river than a place, moving and changing all the time. You can't make rivers flow straight.'

'Don't go through all that again,' she said. 'I'm not trying to make rivers flow straight, I'm trying to get my head straight.'

'You've got to *do* something,' I told her. 'You can't do nothing. Why not go back to your job? You didn't have nightmares when you were working. You were never so unhappy when you were working.'

'I've got to stand back from all that,' she said. 'I'm not sure what any of it means.'

'Fashion,' I said, 'it's all fashion. Fashionable metaphors, fashionable reading, fashionable malaise. What do you care about Jung, for example? You've read twelve pages in a month.'

'Don't go on,' she pleaded, 'you know it leads nowhere.'

But I went on.

'You've never been anywhere,' I told her, 'you've never done anything. You're a nice girl without even the blessing of an unhappy childhood. Your sentimental Buddhism, this junk-shop mysticism, joss-stick therapy, magazine astrology ... none of it is yours, you've worked none of it out for yourself. You fell into it, you fell into a swamp of respectable intuitions. You haven't the originality or passion to intuit anything yourself beyond your own unhappiness. Why are you filling your mind with other people's mystic banalities and giving yourself nightmares?' I got out of bed, opened the curtains and began to get dressed.

'You talk like this was a fiction seminar,' Maisie said. 'Why are you trying to make things worse for me?' Self-pity began to well up from inside her, but she fought it down. 'When you are talking,' she went on, 'I can feel myself, you know, being screwed up like a piece o paper.'

'Perhaps we *are* in a fiction seminar,' I said grimly. Maisie sat up in bed staring at her lap. Suddenly her tone changed. She patted the pillow beside her and said softly,

'Come over here. Come and sit here. I want to touch you, I want you to touch me ...' But I was sighing, and already on my way to the kitchen.

In the kitchen I made myself some coffee and took it through to my study. It had occurred to me in my night of broken sleep that a possible clue to the disappearance of M might be found in the pages of geometry. I had always skipped through them before because mathematics does not interest me. On the Monday, December 5th, 1898, M and my great-grandfather discussed the *vescia piscis*, which apparently is the subject of Euclid's first proposition and a profound influence on the ground plans of many ancient religious buildings. I read through the account of the conversation carefully, trying to understand as best I could the geometry of it. Then, turning the page, I found a lengthy anecdote which M told my great-grandfather that same evening when the coffee had been brought in and the cigars were lit. Just as I was beginning to read Maisie came in.

'And what about you,' she said, as if there had not been an hour break in our exchange, 'all you have is books. Crawling over the past like a fly on a turd.'

I was angry, of course, but I smiled and said cheerfully, 'Crawling? Well, at least I'm moving.'

'You don't speak to me any more,' she said, 'you play me like a pinball machine, for points.'

'Good morning, Hamlet,' I replied, and sat in my chair waiting patiently for what she had to say next. But she did not speak, she left, closing the study door softly behind her.

'In September 1870,' M began to tell my great-grand-father,

I came into the possession of certain documents which not only invalidate everything fundamental to our science of solid geometry but also undermine the whole canon of our physical laws and force one to redefine one's place in Nature's scheme. These papers outweigh in importance the combined work of Marx and Darwin. They were entrusted to me by a young American mathematician, and they are the work of David Hunter, a mathematician too and a Scotsman. The American's name was Goodman. I had corresponded with his father over a number of years in connection with his work on the cyclical theory of menstruation which, incredibly enough, is still widely discredited in this country. I met the young Goodman in Vienna where, along with Hunter and mathematicians from a dozen countries, he had been attending an international conference on mathematics. Goodman was pale and greatly disturbed when I met him, and planned to return to America the following day even though the conference was not yet half complete. He gave the papers into my care with instructions that I was to deliver them to David Hunter if I was ever to learn of his whereabouts. And then, only after much persuasion and insistence on my part, he told me what he had witnessed on the third day of the conference. The conference met every morning at nine thirty when a paper was read and a general discussion ensued. At eleven o'clock refreshments were brought in and many of the mathematicians would get up from the long, highly polished table round which they were all gathered and stroll about the large, elegant room and engage in informal discussions with their colleagues. Now, the conference lasted two weeks, and by a long-standing arrangement the most eminent of the mathematicians read their papers first, followed by the slightly less eminent, and and so on, in a descending hierarchy throughout the two weeks, which caused, as it is wont to do among highly intelligent men, occasional but intense jealousies. Hunter, though a brilliant mathematician, was young and virtually unknown outside his university, which was Edinburgh. He had applied to deliver what he described as a very important paper on solid geometry, and since he was of little account in this pantheon he was assigned to read to the conference on the last day but one, by which time many of the most important figures would have returned to their respective countries. And so on the third morning, as the servants were bringing in the refreshments, Hunter stood up suddenly and addressed his colleagues just as they were rising from their seats. He was a large, shaggy man and, though young, he had about him a certain presence which reduced the hum of conversation to a complete silence.

'Gentlemen,' said Hunter, 'I must ask you to forgive this improper form of address, but I have something to tell you of the utmost importance. I have discovered the plane without a surface.' Amid derisive smiles and gentle bemused laughter, Hunter picked up from the table a large white sheet of paper. With a pocket-knife he made an incision along its surface about three inches long and slightly to one side of its centre. Then he made some rapid, complicated folds and, holding the paper aloft so all could see, he appeared to draw one corner of it through the incision, and as he did so it disappeared.

'Behold, gentlemen,' said Hunter, holding out his empty hands towards the company, 'the plane without a surface.'

Maisie came into my room, washed now and smelling faintly of perfumed soap. She came and stood behind my chair and placed her hands on my shoulders.

'What are you reading?' she said.

'Just bits of the diary which I haven't looked at before.' She began to massage me gently at the base of my neck. I would have found it soothing if it had still been the first year of our marriage. But it was the sixth year and it generated a kind of tension which communicated itself the length of my spine. Maisie wanted something. To restrain her I placed my right hand on her left, and, mistaking this for affection, she leaned forward and kissed under my ear. Her breath smelled of toothpaste and toast. She tugged at my shoulder.

'Let's go in the bedroom,' she whispered. 'We haven't made love for nearly two weeks now.'

'I know,' I replied. 'You know how it is ... with my work.' I felt no desire for Maisie or any other woman. All I wanted to do was turn the next page of my great-grand-father's diary. Maisie took her hands off my shoulders and stood by my side. There was such a sudden ferocity in her silence that I found myself tensing like a sprinter on the starting line. She stretched forward and picked up the sealed jar containing Capt. Nicholls. As she lifted it his penis drifted dreamily from one end of the glass to the other.

'You're so COMPLACENT,' Maisie shrieked, just before she hurled the glass bottle at the wall in front of my table. Instinctively I covered my face with my hands to shield off the shattering glass. As I opened my eyes I heard myself saying,

'Why did you do that? That belonged to my great-grandfather.' Amid the broken glass and the rising stench of formaldehyde lay Capt. Nicholls, slouched across the leather covers of a volume of the diary, grey, limp and menacing, transformed from a treasured curiosity into a horrible obscenity.

'That was a terrible thing to do. Why did you do that?' I said again.

'I'm going for a walk,' Maisie replied, and slammed the door this time as she left the room.

I did not move from my chair for a long time. Maisie had destroyed an object of great value to me. It had stood in his study while he lived, and then it had stood in mine, linking my life with his. I picked a few splinters of glass from my lap and stared at the 160-year-old piece of another human on my table. I looked at it and thought of all the homunculi which had swarmed down its length. I thought of all the places it had been, Cape Town, Boston, Jerusalem, travelling in the dark, fetid inside of Capt. Nicholls's leather breeches, emerging occasionally into the dazzling sunlight to discharge urine in some jostling public place. I thought also of all the things it had touched, all the molecules, of Captain Nicholls's exploring hands on lonely unrequited nights at sea, the sweating walls of cunts of young girls and old whores, their molecules must still exist today, a fine dust blowing from Cheapside to Leicestershire. Who knows how long it might have lasted in its glass jar. I began to clear up the mess. I brought the rubbish bucket in from the kitchen. I swept and picked up all the glass I could find and swabbed up the formaldehyde. Then, holding him by just one end, I tried to ease Capt. Nicholls on to a sheet of newspaper. My stomach heaved as the foreskin began to come away in my fingers. Finally, with my eyes closed, I succeeded, and wrapping him carefully in the newspaper, I carried him into the garden and buried him under the geraniums. All this time I tried to prevent my resentment towards Maisie filling my mind. I wanted to continue with M's story. Back in my chair I dabbed at a few spots of formaldehyde which had blotted the ink, and read on.

For as long as a minute the room was frozen, and with each successive second it appeared to freeze harder. The first to speak was Dr Stanley Rose of Cambridge University, who had much to lose by Hunter's plane without a surface. His reputation, which was very considerable indeed, rested upon his 'Principles of Solid Geometry'.

'How dare you, sir. How dare you insult the dignity of this assembly with a worthless conjuror's trick.' And bolstered by the rising murmur of concurrence behind him, he added, 'You should be ashamed, young man, thoroughly ashamed.' With that, the room erupted like a volcano. With the exception of young Goodman, and of the servants who still stood by with the refreshments, the whole room turned on Hunter and directed at him a senseless babble of denunciation, invective and threat. Some thumped on the table in their fury, others waved their clenched fists. One very frail German gentlemen fell to the floor in an apoplexy and had to be helped to a chair. And there stood Hunter, firm and outwardly unmoved, his head inclined slightly to one side, his fingers resting lightly on the surface of the long polished table. That such an uproar should follow a worthless conjuror's trick clearly demonstrated the extent of the underlying unease, and Hunter surely appreciated this. Raising his hand, and the company falling suddenly silent once more, he said,

'Gentlemen, your concern is understandable and I will effect another proof, the ultimate proof.' This said, he sat down and removed his shoes, stood up and removed his jacket, and then called for a volunteer to assist him, at which Goodman came forward. Hunter strode through the crowd to a couch which stood along one of the walls, and while he settled himself upon it he told the mystified Goodman that when he returned to England he should take with him Hunter's papers and keep them there until he came to collect them. When the mathematicians had gathered round the couch Hunter rolled on to his stomach and clasped his hands behind his back in a strange posture to fashion a hoop with his arms. He asked Goodman to hold his arms in that position for him, and rolled on his side where he began a number of strenuous jerking movements which enabled him to pass one of his feet through the hoop. He asked his assistant to turn him on his other side, where he performed the same movements again and succeeded in passing his other foot between his arms, and at the same time bent his trunk in such a way that his head was able to pass through the hoop in the opposite direction to his feet. With the help of his assistant he began to pass his legs and head past each other through the hoop made by his arms. It was then that the distinguished assembly vented, as one man, a single yelp of utter incredulity. Hunter was beginning to disappear, and now, as his legs and head passed through his arms with greater facility, seemed even to be drawn through by some invisible power, he was almost gone. And now ... he was gone, quite gone, and nothing remained.

M's story put my great-grandfather in a frenzy of excitement. In his diary that night he recorded how he tried 'to prevail upon my guest to send for the papers upon the instant' even though it was by now two o'clock in the morning. M, however, was more sceptical about the whole thing. 'Americans', he told my great-grandfather, 'often indulge in fantastic tales.' But he agreed to bring along the papers the following day. As it turned out M did not dine with my great-grandfather that night because of another engagement, but he called round in the late afternoon with the papers. Before he left he told my great-grandfather he had been through them a number of times and 'there was no sense to be had out of them'. He did not realize then how much he was underestimating my great-grandfather as an amateur mathematician. Over a glass of sherry in front of the drawing-room fire the two men arranged to dine together again at the end of the week, on Saturday. For the next three days my great-grandfather hardly paused from his reading of Hunter's theorems to eat or sleep. The diary is full of nothing else. The pages are covered with scribbles, diagrams and symbols. It seems that Hunter had to devise a new set of symbols, virtually a whole new language, to express his ideas. By the end of the second day my great-grandfather had made his first breakthrough. At the bottom of a page of mathematical scribble he wrote, 'Dimensionality is a function of consciousness'. Turning to the entry for the next day I read the words, 'It disappeared in my hands'. He had re-established the plane without a surface. And there, spread out in front of me, were step by step instructions on how to fold the piece of paper. Turning the next page I suddenly understood the mystery of M's disappearance. Undoubtedly encouraged by my great-grandfather, he had taken part that evening in a scientific experiment, probably in a spirit of great scepticism. For here my great-grandfather had drawn a series of small sketches illustrating what at first glance looked like yoga positions. Clearly they were the secret of Hunter's disappearing act.

My hands were trembling as I cleared a space on my desk. I selected a clean sheet of typing paper and laid it in front of me. I fetched a razor blade from the bathroom. I rummaged in a drawer and found an old pair of compasses, sharpened a pencil and fitted it in. I searched through the house till I found an accurate steel ruler I had once used for fitting window panes, and then I was ready. First I had to cut the paper to size. The piece that Hunter had so casually picked up from the table had obviously been carefully prepared beforehand. The length of the sides had to express a specific ratio. Using the compasses I found the centre of the paper and through this point I drew a line parallel to one of the sides and continued it right to the edge. Then I had to construct a rectangle whose measurements bore a particular relation to those of the sides of the paper. The centre of this rectangle occurred on the line in such a way as to dissect it by the Golden Mean. From the top of this rectangle I drew intersecting arcs, again of specified proportionate radii. This operation was repeated at the lower end of the rectangle, and when the two points of intersection were joined I had the line of incision. Then I started work on the folding lines. Each line seemed to express, in its length, angle of incline and point of intersection with other lines, some mysterious inner harmony of numbers. As I intersected arcs, drew lines and made folds, I felt I was blindly operating a system of the highest, most terrifying form of knowledge, the mathematics of the Absolute. By the time I had made the final fold the piece of paper was the shape of a geometric flower with three concentric rings arranged round the incision at the centre. There was something so tranquil and perfect about this design, something so remote and compelling, that as I stared into it I felt myself going into a light trance and my mind becoming clear and inactive. I shook my head and glanced away. It was time now to turn the flower in on itself and pull it through the incision. This was a delicate operation and now my hands were trembling again. Only by staring into the centre of the design could I calm myself. With my thumbs I began to push the sides of the paper flower towards the centre, and as I did so I felt a numbness settle over the back of my skull. I pushed a little further, the paper glowed whiter for an instant and then it *seemed* to disappear. I say 'seemed' because at first I could not be sure whether I could feel it still in my hands and not see it, or see it but not feel it, or whether I could sense it had disappeared while its external properties remained. The numbness had spread right across my head and shoulders. My senses seemed inadequate to grasp what was happening. 'Dimensionality is a function of consciousness,' I thought. I brought my hands together and there was nothing between them, but even when I opened them again and saw nothing I could not be sure the paper flower had completely gone. An impression remained, an after-image not on the retina but on the mind itself. Just then the door opened behind me, and Maisie said,

'What are you doing?'

I returned as if from a dream to the room and to the faint smell of formaldehyde. It was a long, long time ago now, the destruction of Capt. Nicholls, but the smell revived my resentment, which spread through me like the numbness. Maisie slouched in the doorway, muffled in a thick coat and woollen scarf. She seemed a long way off, and as I looked at her my resentment merged into a familiar weariness of our marriage. I thought, why did she break the glass? Because she wanted to make love? Because she wanted a penis? Because she was jealous of my work, and wanted to smash the connection it had with my great-grandfather's life?

'Why did you do it?' I said out loud, involuntarily. Maisie snorted. She had opened the door and found me hunched over my table staring at my hands.

'Have you been sitting there all afternoon,' she asked, 'thinking about *that*?' She giggled. 'What happened to it, anyway? Did you suck it off?'

'I buried it,' I said, 'under the geraniums.'

She came into the room a little way and said in a serious tone, 'I'm sorry about that, I really am. I just did it before I knew what was happening. Do you forgive me?' I hesitated, and then, because my weariness had blossomed into a sudden resolution, I said,

'Yes, of course I forgive you. It was only a prick in pickle,' and we both laughed. Maisie came over to me and kissed me, and I returned the kiss, prising open her lips with my tongue.

'Are you hungry?' she said, when we were done with kissing. 'Shall I make some supper?'

'Yes,' I said. 'I would love that.' Maisie kissed me on the

top of my head and left the room, while I turned back to my studies, resolving to be as kind as I possibly could to Maisie that evening.

Later we sat in the kitchen eating the meal Maisie had cooked and getting mildly drunk on a bottle of wine. We smoked a joint, the first one we had had together in a very long time. Maisie told me how she was going to get a job with the Forestry Commission planting trees in Scotland next summer. And I told Maisie about the conversation M and my great-grandfather had had about *a posteriori*, and about my great-grandfather's theory that there could not be more than the prime number seventeen positions for making love. We both laughed, and Maisie squeezed my hand, and lovemaking hung in the air between us, in the warm fug of the kitchen. Then we put our coats on and went for a walk. It was almost a full moon. We walked along the main road which runs outside our house and then turned down a narrow street of tightly packed houses with immaculate and minute front gardens. We did not talk much, but our arms were linked and Maisie told me how very stoned and happy she was. We came to a small park which was locked and we stood outside the gates looking up at the moon through the almost leafless branches. When we came home Maisie took a leisurely hot bath while I browsed in my study, checking on a few details. Our bedroom is a warm, comfortable room, luxurious in its way. The bed is seven foot by eight, and I made it myself in the first year of our marriage. Maisie made the sheets, dyed them a deep, rich blue and embroidered the pillow cases. The only light in the room shone through a rough old goatskin lampshade Maisie bought from a man who came to the door. It was a long time since I had taken an interest in the bedroom. We lay side by side in the tangle of sheets and rugs, Maisie voluptuous and drowsy after her bath and stretched full out, and I propped up on my elbow. Maisie said sleepily,

'I was walking along the river this afternoon. The trees are beautiful now, the oaks, the elms ... there are two copper beeches about a mile past the footbridge, you should see them now ... ahh, that feels good.' I had eased her on to her belly and was caressing her back as she spoke. 'There are blackberries, the biggest ones I've ever seen, growing all along the path, and elderberries, too. I'm going to make some wine this autumn ...' I leaned over her and kissed the nape of her neck and brought her arms behind her back. She liked to be manipulated in this way and she submitted warmly. 'And the river is really still,' she was saying. 'You know, reflecting the trees, and the leaves are dropping into the river. Before the winter comes we should go there together, by the river, in the leaves. I found this little place. No one goes there ...' Holding Maisie's arms in position with one hand, I worked her legs towards the 'hoop' with the other. '... I sat in this place for half an hour without moving, like a tree. I saw a water-rat running along the opposite bank, and different kinds of ducks landing on the river and taking off. I heard these plopping noises in the river but I didn't know what they were and I saw two orange butterflies, they almost came on my hand.' When I had her legs in place Maisie said, 'Position number eighteen,' and we both laughed softly. 'Let's go there tomorrow, to the river,' said Maisie as I carefully eased her head towards her arms. 'Careful, careful, that hurts,' she suddenly shouted, and tried to struggle. But it was too late now, her head and legs were in place in the hoop of her arms, and I was beginning to push them through, past each other. 'What's happening?' cried Maisie. Now the positioning of her limbs expressed the breathtaking beauty, the nobility of the human form, and, as in the paper flower, there was a fascinating power in its symmetry. I felt the trance coming on again and the numbness settling over the back of my head. As I drew her arms and legs through, Maisie appeared to turn in on herself like a sock. 'Oh God,' she sighed, 'what's happening?' and her voice sounded very far away. Then she was gone ... and not gone. Her voice was quite tiny, 'What's happening?' and all that remained was the echo of her question above the deep-blue sheets.

Last Day of Summer

I am twelve and lying near-naked on my belly out on the back lawn in the sun when for the first time I hear her laugh. I don't know, I don't move, I just close my eyes. It's a girl's laugh, a young woman's, short and nervous like laughing at nothing funny. I got half my face in the grass I cut an hour before and I can smell the cold soil beneath it. There's a faint breeze coming off the river, the late afternoon sun stinging my back and that laugh jabbing at me like it's all one thing, one taste in my head. The laughing stops and all I can hear is the breeze flapping the pages of my comic, Alice crying somewhere upstairs and a kind of summer heaviness all over the garden. Then I hear them walking across the lawn towards me and I sit up so quickly it makes me dizzy, and the colours have gone out of everything. And there's this fat woman, or girl, walking towards me with my brother. She's so fat her arms can't hang right from her shoulders. She's got rubber tyres round her neck. They're both looking at me and talking about me, and when they get really close I stand up and she shakes my hand and still looking right at me she makes a kind of yelping noise like a polite horse. It's the noise I heard just now, her laugh. Her hand is hot and wet and pink like a sponge, with dimples at the base of each finger. My brother introduces her as Jenny. She's going to take the attic bedroom. She's got a very large face, round like a red moon, and thick glasses which make her eyes as big as golf balls. When she lets go of my hand I can't think of one thing to say. But my brother Peter talks on and on, he tells her what vegetables we are growing and what flowers, he makes her stand where she can get a view of the river between the trees and then he leads her back to the house. My brother is exactly twice my age and he's good at that sort of thing, just talking.

Jenny takes the attic. I've been up there a few times looking for things in the old boxes, or watching the river out of the small window. There's nothing much in the boxes really, just cloth scraps and dressmaking patterns. Perhaps some of them actually belonged to my mother. In one corner there's a pile of picture frames without pictures. Once I was up there because it was raining outside, and downstairs there was a row going on between Peter and some of the others. I helped José clear out the place ready for a bedroom. José used to be Kate's boyfriend and then last spring he moved his things out of Kate's bedroom and moved into the spare room next to mine. We carried the boxes and frames to the garage, we stained the wooden floor black and put down rugs. We took apart the extra bed in my room and carried it up. With that, a table and a chair, a small cupboard and the sloping ceiling, there is just room for two people standing up. All Jenny has for luggage is a small suitcase and a carrier bag. I take them up to her room for her and she follows, breathing harder and harder and stopping half way up the third set of stairs to get a rest. My brother Peter comes up behind and we squeeze in as if we are all going to be living there and we're seeing it for the first time. I point out the window for her so she can see the river. Jenny sits with her big elbows on the table. Sometimes she dabs at her damp red face with a

large white handkerchief while she's listening to some
story of Peter's. I'm sitting on the bed behind her looking
at how immense her back is, and under her chair I can see
her thick pink legs, how they taper away and squeeze into
tiny shoes at the bottom. Everywhere she's pink. The smell
of her sweat fills the room. It smells like the new cut grass
outside, and I get this idea that I mustn't breathe it in too
deeply or I'll get fat too. We stand up to go so she can get
on with her unpacking and she's saying thank you for
everything, and as I go through the door she makes her
little yelp, her nervous laugh. Without meaning to I
glance back at her through the doorway and she's looking
right at me with her magnified golf-balls eyes.

'You don't say much, do you?' she says. Which sort of
makes it even harder to think of something to say. So I just
smile at her and carry on down the stairs.

Downstairs it's my turn to help Kate cook the supper.
Kate is tall and slim and sad. Really the opposite of Jenny.
When I have girl friends I'm going to have them like Kate.
She's very pale, though, even at this time in the summer.
She has strange-coloured hair. Once I heard Sam say it
was the colour of a brown envelope. Sam is one of Peter's
friends who also lives here and who wanted to move his
things into Kate's bedroom when José moved his out. But
Kate is sort of haughty and she doesn't like Sam because
he's too noisy. If Sam moved into Kate's room he'd always
be waking up Alice, Kate's little girl. When Kate and José
are in the same room I always watch them to see if they
ever look at each other, and they never do. Last April I
went into Kate's room one afternoon to borrow something
and she and José were in bed asleep. José's parents come
from Spain and his skin is very dark. Kate was lying on her
back with one arm stretched out, and José was lying on her
arm, snuggling up to her side. They didn't have pyjamas on,

and the sheet came up to their waists. They were so black and so white. I stood at the foot of the bed a long time, watching them. It was like some secret I'd found out. Then Kate opened her eyes and saw me there and told me very softly to get out. It seems pretty strange to me that they were lying there like that and now they don't even look at each other. That wouldn't happen with me if I was lying on some girl's arm. Kate doesn't like cooking. She has to spend a lot of time making sure Alice doesn't put knives in her mouth or pull boiling pots off the stove. Kate prefers dressing-up and going out, or talking for hours on the telephone, which is what I would rather do if I was a girl. Once she stayed out late and my brother Peter had to put Alice to bed. Kate always looks sad when she speaks to Alice, when she's telling her what to do she speaks very softly as if she doesn't really want to be speaking to Alice at all. And it's the same when she talks to me, as if it's not really talking at all. When she sees my back in the kitchen she takes me through to the downstairs bathroom and dabs calamine lotion over me with a piece of cotton wool. I can see her in the mirror, she doesn't seem to have any particular expression on her face. She makes a sound between her teeth, half a whistle and half a sigh, and when she wants a different part of my back towards the light she pushes or pulls me about by my arm. She asks me quickly and quietly what the girl upstairs is like, and when I tell her, 'She's very fat and she's got a funny laugh,' she doesn't make any reply. I cut up vegetables for Kate and lay the table. Then I walk down to the river to look at my boat. I bought it with some money I got when my parents died. By the time I get to the jetty it's past sunset and the river is black with scraps of red like the cloth scraps that used to be in the attic. Tonight the river is slow and the air is warm and smooth. I don't untie the boat, my back is too

sore from the sun to row. Instead I climb in and sit with
the quiet rise and fall of the river, watching the red cloth
sink in the black water and wondering if I breathed in too
much of Jenny's smell.

When I get back they are about to start eating. Jenny is
sitting next to Peter and when I come in she doesn't look
up from her plate, even when I sit down on the other side
of her. She's so big beside me, and yet so bowed down over
her plate, looking as if she doesn't really want to exist, that
I feel sorry for her in a way and I want to speak to her. But
I can't think of anything to say. In fact no one has anything to say this meal, they're all just pushing their knives
and forks backwards and forwards over their plates, and
now and then someone murmurs for something to be
passed. It doesn't usually happen like this when we're
eating, there's usually something going on. But Jenny's
here, more silent than any of us, and bigger, too, and not
looking up from her plate. Sam clears his throat and looks
down our end of the table at Jenny, and everyone else looks
up too, except for her, waiting for something. Sam clears
his throat again and says,

'Where were you living before, Jenny?' Because no one's
been speaking it comes out flat, as if Sam's in an office
filling in a form for her. And Jenny, still looking down at
her plate, says,

'Manchester.' Then she looks at Sam. 'In a flat.' And
she gives a little yelp of a laugh, probably because we're
all listening and looking at her, and then she sinks back
into her plate while Sam's saying something like, 'Ah, I
see,' and thinking of the next thing to say. Upstairs, Alice
starts crying so Kate goes and brings her down and lets her
sit on her lap. When she stops crying she points at each one
of us in turn and shouts, 'UH, UH, UH,' and so on right
round the table while we all sit there eating and not

speaking. It's like she's telling us off for not thinking of
things to say. Kate tells her to be quiet in the sad way she
always has when she's with Alice. Sometimes I think she's
like that because Alice doesn't have a father. She doesn't
look at all like Kate, she has very fair hair and ears that
are too large for her head. A year or two ago when Alice
was very little I used to think that José was her father. But
his hair is black, and he never pays much attention to
Alice. When everybody's finished the first course and I'm
helping Kate collect the dishes, Jenny offers to have Alice
on her lap. Alice is still shouting and pointing at different
things in the room, but once she's on Jenny's lap she goes
very quiet. Probably because it's the biggest lap she's ever
seen. Kate and I bring in fruit and tea, and when we are
peeling oranges and bananas, eating the apples from our
tree in the garden, pouring tea and passing cups with milk
and sugar round, everyone starts talking and laughing like
they usually do, like there never was anything holding
them back. And Jenny is giving Alice a really good time on
her lap, making her knees gallop like a horse, making her
hand swoop down like a bird on to Alice's belly, showing
her tricks with her fingers, so that all the time Alice is
shouting for more. It's the first time I've heard her laugh
like that. And then Jenny glances down the table at Kate
who's been watching them play with the same kind of look
she might have on her face if she was watching the telly.
Jenny carries Alice to her mother like she's suddenly
feeling guilty about having Alice on her lap for such a
long time and having so much fun. Alice is shouting,
'More, more, more,' when she's back at the other end of
the table, and she's still shouting it five minutes later when
her mother carries her up to bed.

　　Because my brother asks me to, I take coffee up to
Jenny's room early next morning. When I go in she's

already up, sitting at her table putting stamps on letters. She looks smaller than she did last night. She has her window wide open and her room is full of morning air, it feels like she's been up for a long time. Out of her window I can see the river stretching between the trees, light and quiet in the sun. I want to get outside, I want to see my boat before breakfast. But Jenny wants to talk. She makes me sit on her bed and tell her about myself. She doesn't ask me any questions and since I'm not sure how to start off telling someone about myself I sit there and watch while she writes addresses on her letters and sips her coffee. But I don't mind, it's all right in Jenny's room. She's put two pictures on the wall. One is a framed photograph taken in a zoo of a monkey walking upside down along a branch with its baby hanging on to its stomach. You can tell it is a zoo because in the bottom corner there's a zoo-keeper's cap and part of his face. The other is a colour picture taken out of a magazine of two children running along the sea shore holding hands. The sun is setting and everything in the picture is deep red, even the children. It's a very good picture. She finishes with her letters and asks me where I go to school. I tell her about the new school I'm going to when the holidays are over, the big comprehensive in Reading. But I haven't been there yet, so there isn't much I can tell her about it. She sees me looking out the window again.

'Are you going down to the river?'

'Yes, I have to see my boat.'

'Can I come with you? Will you show me the river?' I wait for her by the door, watching her squeeze her round, pink feet into small, flat shoes and brush her very short hair with a brush which has a mirror on the back. We walk across the lawn to the kissing gate at the bottom of the garden and along the path through the high ferns.

Half way down I stop to listen to a yellow-hammer, and she tells me that she doesn't know the song of one bird. Most grown-up people will never tell you that they don't know things. So farther on down the path just before it opens out on to the jetty we stop under an old oak tree so she can hear a blackbird. I know there's one up there, it's always up there singing this time in the morning. Just as we get there it stops and we have to wait quietly for it to begin again. Standing by that half-dead old trunk I can hear other birds in other trees and the river just round the corner washing under the jetty. But our bird is taking a rest. Something about waiting in silence makes Jenny nervous and she pinches her nose tight to stop her yelp of a laugh getting out. I want her to hear the blackbird so much I put my hand on her arm, and when I do that she takes her hand away from her nose and smiles. Just a few seconds after that the blackbird sets out on its long complicated song. It was waiting all the time for us to get settled. We walk out on to the jetty and I show her my boat tied up at the end. It's a rowing boat, green on the outside and red on the inside like a fruit. I've been down here every day all this summer to row it, paint it, wipe it down, and sometimes just to look at it. Once I rowed it seven miles upstream and spent the rest of the day drifting back down. We sit on the edge of the jetty looking at my boat, the river and the trees on the other side. Then Jenny looks downstream and says,

'London's down there.' London is a terrible secret I try to keep from the river. It doesn't know about it yet while it's flowing past our house. So I just nod and say nothing. Jenny asks me if she can sit in the boat. It worries me at first that she's going to be too heavy. But of course I cannot tell her that. I lean over the jetty and hold the painter rope for her to climb in. She does it with a lot of grunting and rocking around. And since the boat doesn't look any lower now than it usually does, I get in too and we watch the river from this new level where you can see how strong and old it really is. We sit talking for a long time. First I tell her about how my parents died two years ago in a car crash and how my brother had ideas for turning the house into a kind of commune. At first he was going to have over twenty people living here. But now I think he wants to keep it down to about eight. Then Jenny tells me about the time she was a teacher in a big school in Manchester where all the children were always laughing at her because she was fat. She doesn't seem to mind talking about it, though. She has some funny stories of her time there. When she's telling me of the time when the children locked her in a book cupboard we both laugh so much the boat rocks from side to side and pushes small waves out into the river. This time Jenny's laugh is easy and kind of rhythmic, not hard and yelping like before. On the way back she recognizes two blackbirds by their songs, and when we're crossing the lawn she points out another. I just nod. It's a song-thrush really, but I'm too hungry to tell her the difference.

Three days later I hear Jenny singing. I'm in the back yard trying to put together a bicycle out of bits and pieces and I hear her through the open kitchen window. She's in there cooking lunch and looking after Alice while Kate visits friends. It's a song she doesn't know the words for, half way between happy and sad, and she's singing like an old croaky Negress to Alice. New morning man la-la, la-la-la-, l'la, new morning man la-la-la, la-la, l'la, new morning man take me 'way from here. That afternoon I row her out on the river and she has another song with the same kind of tune, but this time with no words at all. Ya-la-la, ya-laaa, ya-eeeee. She spreads her hands out and

rolls her big magnified eyes around like it's a serenade
especially for me. A week later Jenny's songs are all over
the house, sometimes with a line or two if she can remember it, most often with no words at all. She spends a
lot of her time in the kitchen and that's where she does
most of her singing. Somehow she makes more space in
there. She scrapes paint off the north window to let in
more light. No one can think why it was painted over in the
first place. She carries out an old table, and when it's out
everyone realizes that it was always in the way. One
afternoon she paints the whole of one wall white to make
the kitchen look bigger, and she arranges the pots and
plates so that you always know where they are and even I
can reach them. She makes it into the kind of kitchen you
can sit around in when you've got nothing else to do. Jenny
makes her own bread and bakes cakes, things we usually go
to the shop for. On the third day she's here I find clean
sheets on my bed. She takes the sheets I've been using all
summer and most of my clothes away for washing. She
spends all of one afternoon making a curry, and that night
I eat the best meal in two years. When the others tell her
how good they think it is Jenny gets nervous and does her
yelping laugh. I can see the others are still bothered when
she does it, they sort of look away as if it is something
disgusting that would be rude to look at. But it doesn't
worry me at all when she does that laugh, I don't even
hear it except when the others are there at the table
looking away. Most afternoons we go out on the river
together and I try to teach her to row, and listen to her
stories of when she was teaching, and when she was
working in a supermarket, how she used to watch old
people come in each day to shoplift bacon and butter. I
teach her some more birdsongs, but the only one she can
really remember is the first one, the blackbird. In her

room she shows me pictures of her parents and her brother
and she says,

'I'm the only fat one.' I show her some pictures of my
parents, too. One of them was taken a month before they
died, and in it they are walking down some steps holding
hands and laughing at something outside the picture. They
were laughing at my brother who was fooling around to
make them laugh for the picture I was taking. I had just
got the camera for my tenth birthday and that was one of
the first pictures I took with it. Jenny looks at it for a long
time and says something about her looking like a very nice
woman, and suddenly I see my mother as just a woman in
a picture, it could be any woman, and for the first time
she's far off, not in my head looking out, but outside my
head being looked at by me, Jenny or anyone who picks up
the photo. Jenny takes it out of my hand and puts it away
with the others in the shoe box. As we go downstairs she
starts off on a long story about a friend of hers who was
producing a play which ended strangely and quietly. The
friend wanted Jenny to start off the clapping at the end but
Jenny got it all wrong somehow and started everyone
clapping fifteen minutes before the end during a quiet bit
so that the last part of the play was lost and the clapping
was all the louder because no one knew what the play was
about. All this, I suppose, is to make me stop thinking
about my mother, which it does.

Kate spends more time with her friends in Reading. One
morning I'm in the kitchen when she comes in very
smartly dressed in a kind of leather suit and high leather
boots. She sits down opposite me to wait for Jenny to come
down so she can tell her what food to give Alice that day,
and what time she'll be back. It reminds me of another
morning almost two years ago when Kate came into the
kitchen in the same kind of suit. She sat down at the table,

undid her blouse and started to knead with her fingers blueish-white milk into a bottle from one tit and then the other. She didn't seem to notice me sitting there.

'What are you doing that for?' I asked her.

She said, 'It's for Janet to give to Alice later on today. I've got to go out.' Janet was a black girl who used to be living here. It was strange watching Kate milk herself into a bottle. It made me think how we're just animals with clothes on doing very peculiar things, like monkeys at a tea party. But we get so used to each other most of the time. I wonder if Kate is thinking of that time now, sitting with me in the kitchen first thing in the morning. She's got orange lipstick on and her hair tied back and that makes her look even thinner than usual. Her lipstick is sort of fluorescent, like a road sign. Every minute she looks at her watch and her leather creaks. She looks like some beautiful woman from outer space. Then Jenny comes down, wearing a huge old dressing-gown made out of patches and yawning because she's just got out of bed, and Kate speaks to her very quickly and quietly about Alice's food for the day. It's as if it makes her sad, talking about that sort of thing. She picks up her bag and runs out the kitchen and calls, ''Bye,' over her shoulder. Jenny sits down at the table and drinks tea and it's like she really is the big mama left behind at home to look after the rich lady's daughter. Yo' daddy's rich and yo' mama's goodlookin', lah la-la-la la-la don' yo' cry. And there's something in the way the others treat Jenny. Like she's outside things, and not really a person like they are. They've got used to her cooking big meals and making cakes. No one says anything about it now. Sometimes in the evenings Peter, Kate, José and Sam sit around and smoke hashish in Peter's homemade water-pipe and listen to the stereo turned up loud. When they do that Jenny usually goes up to her room, she doesn't like to be with them when they're doing that, and I can see they sort of resent it. And though she's a girl she's not beautiful like Kate or Sharon, my brother's girl friend. She doesn't wear jeans and Indian shirts like they do, either, probably because she can't find any to fit her. She wears dresses with flowers on and ordinary things like my mother or the lady in the post office wear. And when she gets nervous about something and does her laugh I can tell they think of her like some sort of mental patient, I know that by the way they turn their eyes away. And they still think about how fat she is. Sometimes when she's not there Sam calls her Slim Jim, and it always makes the others laugh. It's not that they're unfriendly to her or anything like that, it's just that in some way that's hard to describe they keep her apart from themselves. One time we're out on the river she asks me about hashish.

'What do you think about it all?' she says, and I tell her my brother won't let me try it till I'm fifteen. I know she's dead against it, but she doesn't mention it again. It's that same afternoon I take a photograph of her leaning by the kitchen door holding Alice and squinting a little into the sun. She takes mine too, riding no-hands round the back yard on the bicycle I put together out of bits and pieces.

It's hard to say exactly when Jenny becomes Alice's mother. At first she's just looking after her while Kate visits friends. Then the visits get more often till they are almost every day. So the three of us, Jenny, Alice and me, spend a lot of time together by the river. By the jetty there's a grass bank which slopes down on to a tiny sand beach about six feet across. Jenny sits on the bank playing with Alice while I do things to my boat. When we first put Alice in the boat she squeals like a baby pig. She doesn't trust the water. It's a long time before she'll stand on the small beach, and when she does at last she never takes her eyes off the water's edge to make sure it doesn't creep up on her. But when she sees Jenny waving to her from the boat, and quite safe, she changes her mind and we make a trip to the other side of the river. Alice doesn't mind about Kate being away because she likes Jenny, who sings her the bits of songs she knows and talks to her all the time when they are sitting on the grass bank by the river. Alice does not understand a word of it but she likes the sound of Jenny's voice going on and on. Sometimes Alice points up to Jenny's mouth and says, 'More, more.' Kate is always so quiet and sad with her she doesn't hear many voices speaking right at her. One night Kate stays away and doesn't come back till the next morning. Alice is sitting on Jenny's knee spreading her breakfast across the kitchen table when Kate comes running in, scoops her up, hugs her and asks over and over again without giving anyone time to reply,

'Has she been all right? Has she been all right? Has she been all right?' The same afternoon Alice is back with Jenny because Kate has to go off somewhere again. I'm in the hall outside the kitchen when I hear her tell Jenny she'll be back in the early evening, and a few minutes later I see her walking down the drive carrying a small suitcase. When she gets back two days later she just puts her head round the door to see if Alice is still there, and then she goes up to her room. It's not always such a good thing having Alice with us all the time. We can't go very far in the boat. After twenty minutes Alice gets suspicious of the water again and wants to be back on the shore. And if we want to walk somewhere Alice has to be carried most of the way. It means I can't show Jenny some of my special places along the river. By the end of the day Alice gets pretty miserable, moaning and crying about nothing because she's tired. I get fed up spending so much time with

Alice. Kate stays up in her room most of the day. One afternoon I take her up some tea and she's sitting in a chair asleep. With Alice there so much of the time Jenny and I don't talk together as much as we did when she first came. Not because Alice is listening, but because all Jenny's time is taken up with her. She doesn't think of anything else, really, it seems like she doesn't want to talk with anyone but Alice. One evening we are all sitting around in the front room after supper. Kate is in the hall having a long argument with someone on the telephone. She finishes, comes in, sits down in a noisy kind of way and carries on reading. But I can see she's angry and not really reading at all. No one speaks for a while, then Alice starts crying upstairs and shouting for Jenny. Jenny and Kate both look up at once and stare at each other for a moment. Then Kate gets up and leaves the room. We all pretend to go on reading but really we are listening to Kate's footsteps on the stairs. We hear her walk into Alice's room, which is right over this one, and we hear Alice shout louder and louder for Jenny to come up. Kate comes back down the stairs, this time quickly. When she comes in the room Jenny looks up and they stare at each other again. And all the time Alice goes on shouting for Jenny. Jenny gets up and squeezes past Kate at the door. They don't speak. The rest of us, Peter, Sam, José and me, we carry on with our pretend reading and listen to Jenny's footsteps upstairs. The crying stops and she stays up there a long time. When she comes down Kate is back in her chair with her magazine. Jenny sits down and no one looks up, no one speaks.

Suddenly the summer is over. Jenny comes into my room early one morning to drag the sheets off my bed and all the clothes she can find in the room. Everything has to be washed before I go to school. Then she gets me to clean out my room, all the old comics and plates and cups which have been collecting under my bed all summer, all the dust and the pots of paint I've been using on my boat. She finds a small table in the garage and I help her carry it to my room. It's going to be my desk for doing homework on. She takes me into the village for a treat, and she won't tell me what it is. When we get there it turns out to be a haircut. I'm about to walk away when she puts her hand on my shoulder.

'Don't be silly,' she says. 'You can't go to school looking like that, you won't last a day.' So I sit still for the barber and let him cut away my whole summer while Jenny sits behind me, laughing at me scowling at her in the mirror. She gets some money from my brother Peter and takes me on the bus into town to buy a school uniform. It's strange having her tell me what to do all of a sudden after our times out on the river. But I don't mind, really, I can't think of any good reasons for not doing the things she says. She steers me through the main shopping streets, into shoe shops and outfitters, she buys me a red blazer and a cap, two pairs of black leather shoes, six pairs of grey socks, two pairs of grey trousers and five grey shirts, and all the time she's saying, 'Do you like these ones? Do you like this?' and since I don't have any special feeling for one particular shade of grey, I agree with whatever she thinks is the best. It's all over in an hour. That evening she empties my drawers of my rock collection to make room for the new clothes, and she gets me to put on the whole uniform. They all laugh downstairs, especially when I put the red cap on. Sam says I look like an inter-galactic postman. For three nights in a row she has me scrubbing my knees with a nail-brush to get the dirt out from under the skin.

Then on Sunday, the day before I start back at school, I go down to the boat with Jenny and Alice for the last time. In the evening I'm going to help Peter and Sam drag my boat up the path and across the lawn into the garage for the winter. Then we're going to build another jetty, a stronger one. It's the last boat trip of the summer. Jenny lifts Alice in and climbs in herself while I hold the boat steady from the jetty. As I'm pushing us off with an oar, Jenny starts one of her songs. Jeeesus won't you come on down, Jeeesus won't you come on down, Jeeesus won't you come on down, lah, la-la-la-lah, la-la. Alice stands between Jenny's knees watching me row. She thinks it's funny, the way I strain backwards and forwards. She thinks it's a game I'm playing with her, moving close up to her face and away again. It's strange, our last day on the river. When Jenny's finished her song no one speaks for a long time. Just Alice laughing at me. It's so still on the river, her laugh carries across the water to nowhere. The sun is a kind of pale yellow like it's burnt out at the end of summer, there's no wind in the trees on the banks, and no birdsong. Even the oars make no sound in the water. I row upstream with the sun on my back, but it's too pale to feel it, it's too pale to make shadows, even. Up ahead there's an old man standing under an oak tree, fishing. When we are level with him he looks up and stares at us in our boat and we stare back at him on the bank. His face does not change when he's looking at us. Our faces do not change, either, no one says hello. He has a long piece of grass in his mouth and when we've passed he takes it out and spits quietly into the river. Jenny trails her hand in the thick water and watches the bank as if it's something she's only seeing in her mind. It makes me think she doesn't really want to be out there on the river with me. She only came because of all the other times we've been rowing together, and because this is the last time this summer. It sort of makes me sad, thinking that, it makes it harder to row. Then after we've been going for about half an hour she looks at me and smiles and I can tell it's all in my head about her not wanting to be on the river because she starts talking about the summer, about all the things we've been doing. She makes it sound really great, much better than it was really. About the long walks we went on, and paddling at the edge of the river with Alice, how I tried to teach her to row and remember different birdsongs, and the times we used to get up while the others were still asleep and row on the river before breakfast. She gets me going too, remembering all the things we did, like the time we thought we saw a waxwing, and another time we waited one evening behind a bush for a badger to come out of its hole. Pretty soon we get really excited about what a summer it's been and the things we're going to do next year, shouting and laughing into the dead air. And then Jenny says,

'And tomorrow you put on your red cap and go to school.' There's something in the way she says it, pretending to be serious and telling me off, with one finger wagging in the air, that makes it the funniest thing I ever heard. And the idea of it too, of doing all those things in the summer and then at the end of it putting on a red cap and going to school. We start laughing and it seems like we're never going to stop. I have to put down the oars. Our hooting and cackling gets louder and louder because the still air doesn't carry it across the water and the noise of it stays with us in the boat. Each time we catch the other's eye we laugh harder and louder till it begins to hurt down my sides, and more than anything I want to stop. Alice starts to cry because she doesn't know what's happening, and that makes us laugh more. Jenny leans over the side of the boat so she can't see me. But her laugh is getting tighter and drier, little hard yelps like pieces of stone from her throat. Her big pink face and her big pink arms are shaking and straining to catch a mouthful of air, but it's all going out of her in little pieces of stone. She leans back into the boat. Her mouth is laughing but her eyes look kind of scared and dry. She drops to her knees, holding her stomach with the pain of laughing, and knocks Alice down with her. And the boat tips over. It tips over because Jenny falls against the side, because Jenny is big and my boat is small. It goes over quickly, like the click of my camera shutter, and suddenly I'm at the deep green bottom of the river touching the cold soft mud with the back of my hand and feeling the reeds on my face. I can hear laughter like sinking pieces of stone by my ear. But when I push upwards to the surface I feel no one near me. When I come up it's dark on the river. I've been down a long time. Something touches my head and I realize I'm inside the upturned boat. I go down again and up the other side. It takes me a long time to get my breath. I work my way round the boat shouting over and over for Jenny and Alice. I put my mouth in the water and shout their names. But no one answers, nothing breaks the surface. I'm the only one on the river. So I hang on to the side of the boat and wait for them to come up. I wait a long time, drifting along with the boat, with the laughter still in my head, watching the river and the yellow patches on it from the sun getting low. Sometimes great shivers run through my legs and back, but mostly I'm calm, hanging on to the green shell with nothing in my mind, nothing at all, just watching the river, waiting for the surface to break and the yellow patches to scatter. I drift past the place where the old man was fishing and it seems like a very long time ago. He's gone now, there's just a paper bag in the place where he was standing. I get so tired I close my eyes and it feels like I'm at home in bed and it's winter and my mother's coming into my room to say goodnight. She turns out the light and I slip off the boat into the river. Then I remember and I shout for Jenny and Alice and watch the river again and my eyes start to close and my mother comes into my room and says goodnight and turns out the light and I sink back into the water again. After a long time I forget to shout for Jenny and Alice, I just hang there and drift down. I'm looking at a place on the bank I used to know very well a long time ago. There's a patch of sand and a grass bank by a jetty. The yellow patches are sinking into the river when I push away from the boat. I let it drift on down to London and I swim slowly through the black water to the jetty.

Cocker at the Theatre

There was dust on the boards, the backdrops were half painted and they were all naked on the stage, with the bright lights to keep them warm and show up the dust in the air. There was nowhere to sit so they shuffled about miserably. They had no pockets to put their hands in, and there were no cigarettes.

'Is this your first time?' It was everybody's first time, only the director knew that. Only friends spoke, softly and not continuously. The rest were silent. How do naked strangers begin a conversation? No one knew. The professional men – for professional reasons – glanced at each other's parts, while the others, friends of friends of the director and needing some cash, regarded the women without appearing to. Jasmin called from the back of the auditorium where he had been talking with the costume designer, he called out in Welsh Camp Cockney,

'Have you all masturbated, boys? Well done.' (No one had spoken.) 'The first hard-on I see and out you go. This is a respectable show.' Some of the women giggled, the unprofessional men wandered out of the lights, two A.S.M.s carried a rolled carpet on stage. They said, 'Mind your backs,' and they all felt more naked than before. A man with a bush hat and a white shirt set up a tape recorder in the pit. He was scornful as he threaded the tape. It was the copulation scene.

'I want G.T.C., Jack,' Jasmin said to him. 'Let them hear it first.' There were four large loudspeakers, there was no escaping.

'Well, you've heard about the privacy of the sex-uu-aal act,
Let me tell you people, just for a fact,
Riiiight acroooss the nay-ay-ation
It's the in-out one-two-three Grand Time Copulation.'

There were soaring violins and a military band, and after the chorus a march in exultant two-time with trombones, snare drums and a glockenspiel. Jasmin came down the aisle towards the stage.

'That's your fucking-music, boys and girls.' He undid the top button of his shirt. He wrote this one himself.

'Where's Dale? I want Dale.' Out of the dark came the choreographer. She had a stylish trenchcoat on, tied in the middle with a wide belt. She had a small waist, sunglasses and a sticky-bun hairdo. She walked like a pair of scissors. Without turning round Jasmin called out to the man who was leaving by a door at the back of the auditorium.

'I *want* those wigs, Harry dear. I *want* those wigs. No wigs, no Harry.' Jasmin sat down in the front row. He made a steeple under his nose with his hands and crossed his legs. Dale climbed on the stage. She stood in the middle of the large carpet spread across the boards, one hand on her hip. She said, 'I want the girls squatting in a V shape, five on each side.' She stood where the apex was to be, moving her arms. They sat at her feet and she clipped up and down the middle leaving a trail of musk. She made the V deeper, then shallow again, she made it a horseshoe and a crescent and then a shallow V once more.

'Very nice, Dale,' said Jasmin. The V pointed backstage. Dale moved a girl from the middle and replaced her with a girl from the edge. She did not speak to them, she took them by the elbow, leading them from this place to that place. They could not see her eyes through her glasses and they did not always know what she wanted. She guided a man across to each woman and pressed on his shoulders to make him sit down opposite. She fitted the legs together of each couple, she straightened their backs, she put their heads in position and made the partners clasp forearms. Jasmin lit a cigarette. There were ten couples in the V shape on the carpet, which really belonged in the foyer.

At last Dale said, 'I am clapping my hands, you are rocking backwards and forwards in time.'

They began to rock like children playing at ships. The director walked to the back of the auditorium.

'I think closer together, darling, it looks like nothing at all from here.' Dale pressed the couples closer together. When they began to move again their pubic hair rasped. It was hard to keep time. It was very much a matter of practice. One couple fell sideways and the girl banged her head on the floor. She rubbed her head and Dale came over and rubbed it too and reassembled them. Jasmin skipped down the aisle.

'We'll try it with the music. Jack, please. And remember, boys and girls, after the singing you go into two-time.'

'Well, you've heard about the privacy of the sex-uu-aal act ...'

The boys and girls began to rock while Dale clapped her hands. One, two, three, four. Jasmin stood half way up the aisle, his arms crossed. He uncrossed them, and screamed,

'Stop. Enough.' It was suddenly very quiet. The couples stared into the blackness beyond the lights and waited. Jasmin came down the steps slowly, and when he reached the stage he spoke softly.

'I know it's hard, but you have to look as if you are enjoying this thing.' (His voice rose.) 'Some people do, you know. It's a fuck, you understand, not a funeral.' (His voice sank.) 'Let's have it again, with some enthusiasm this time. Jack, please.' Dale realigned those units rocked out of position and the director climbed the stairs again. It was better, there was no doubt that this time it was better. Dale stood by Jasmin and watched. He put his hand on her shoulder and smiled at her glasses.

'Darling, it's good, it's going to be good.'

Dale said, 'The two on the end are moving well. If they were all like that I would be out of a job.'

'It's the in-out one-two-three Grand Time Copulation.'

Dale clapped to help them with the new rhythm. Jasmin sat down in the front row and lit a cigarette. He called back to Dale,

'Them on the end ...' She put her finger to her ear to show him she could not hear, and walked down the steps towards him.

'Them on the end, they're going too fast, what do you think?' They watched together. It was true, the two who had been moving well, they were a little out of time. Jasmin made another steeple under his nose and Dale scissored on to the stage. She stood over them and clapped.

'One two, one two,' she shouted. They did not seem to hear Dale, or the trombones, snare drums and glockenspiel.

'One fucking two,' screamed Dale. She appealed to Jasmin. 'I expect them to have some sense of rhythm.'

But Jasmin did not hear because he was screaming too.

'Cut! Stop! Turn that thing off, Jack.' All the couples creaked to a standstill except the couple on the end. Everyone watched the couple on the end, who were rocking faster now. They had their own sinuous rhythm.

'My God,' said Jasmin, 'they're fucking.' He shouted at the A.S.M.s. 'Get them apart, will you, and get those grins off your faces or you won't work in London again.' He shouted at the other couples. 'Clear off, back in half an hour. No, no, stay here.' He turned to Dale, his voice was hoarse. 'I'm sorry about this, darling. I know just how you feel. It's disgusting and obscene, and it's all my fault. I should have checked them all first. It won't happen again.' And while he was talking Dale snipped up the aisle and disappeared. Meanwhile the couple rocked on without music. There was only the creaking of boards beneath the carpet and the woman's low moans. The A.S.M.s stood about, not sure what to do.

'Pull them apart,' Jasmin shouted again. One of the A.S.M.s tugged at the man's shoulders, but they were sweaty and there was nowhere to hold on. Jasmin turned away, tears in his eyes. It was hard to believe. The others were glad of the break, they stood around and watched. The A.S.M. who had tugged at the shoulders brought on a bucket of water. Jasmin blew his nose.

'Don't be pathetic,' he croaked, 'they might as well finish it now.' They juddered to an end as he was speaking. They pushed apart and the girl ran off to the dressing-room, leaving the man standing alone. Jasmin climbed on stage, trembling with sarcasm.

'Well, well, Portnoy, did you get your little poke?

Feeling better now?' The man stood with his hands behind his back. His prick was angry and gluey, it let itself down in little throbs.

'Yes, thank you, Mr Cleaver,' the man said.

'What's your name, dear?'

'Cocker.' Jack snorted in his pit, the closest he ever came to laughing. The rest sucked their lips. Jasmin took a deep breath.

'Well, Cocker, you and the little man stuck on the end of you can crawl off this stage, and take shagging Nellie with you. I hope you find a gutter big enough for two.'

'I'm sure we will, Mr Cleaver, thank you.' Jasmin climbed down into the auditorium.

'Positions, the rest of you,' he said. He sat down. There were days when he could weep, really weep. But he did not, he lit a cigarette.

Butterflies

I saw my first corpse on Thursday. Today it was Sunday
and there was nothing to do. And it was hot. I have never
known it so hot in England. Towards midday I decided
on a walk. I stood outside the house, hesitating. I was not
sure whether to go left or right. Charlie was on the other
side of the street, underneath a car. He must have seen
my legs for he called out,

'How's tricks?' I never have ready answers to questions
like that. I fumbled in my mind for several seconds, and said,

'How are you, Charlie?' He crawled out. The sun was
on my side of the street, straight into his eyes. He shielded
them with his hand, and said,

'Where you off to now?' Again I did not know. It was
Sunday, there was nothing to do, it was too hot ...

'Out,' I said. 'A walk ...' I crossed over and looked at
the car's engine, although it meant nothing to me.
Charlie is an old man who knows about machines. He
repairs cars for the people in the street and their friends.
He came round the side of the car carrying a heavy tool
kit in two hands.

'She died, then?' He stood there wiping a spanner
with cotton waste for something to do. He knew it already,
of course, but he wanted to hear my story.

'Yes,' I told him. 'She's dead.' He waited for me to go

on. I leaned against the side of the car. Its roof was too
hot to touch. Charlie prompted me.

'You saw her last ...'

'I was on the bridge. I saw her running by the canal.'

'You saw her ...'

'I didn't see her fall in.' Charlie put the spanner back in
the box. He was getting ready to crawl back under the car,
his way of telling me the conversation was over. I was still
deciding which way to walk. Before Charlie disappeared
he said,

'Shame, great shame.'

I walked off to the left because that was the way I was
facing. I walked down several streets, between privet
hedges and hot, parked cars. Down each street there was
the same smell of lunch cooking. I heard the same radio
programme through open windows. I saw cats and dogs
but very few people, and only from a distance. I took off
my jacket and carried it over my arm. I wanted to be
near trees and water. There are no parks in this part of
London, only car parks. And there is the canal, the brown
canal which goes between factories and past a scrap heap,
the canal little Jane drowned in. I walked to the public
library. I knew in advance it would be closed but I prefer
to sit on the steps outside. I sat there now, in a shrinking
patch of shade. A hot wind was blowing down the street.
It stirred the litter round my feet. I watched a sheet of
newspaper blown along the centre of the road, a piece out
of the *Daily Mirror*. It stopped and I could read a part of a
headline ... 'MAN WHO' ... There was nobody about.
Round the corner I heard the tinkle of an ice-cream van
and I realized I was thirsty. It was playing something out
of a Mozart piano sonata. It stopped abruptly, in the
middle of a note, as if someone had kicked the machine. I
walked quickly up the street but when I got to the corner

it had gone. A moment later I heard it again, and it sounded a long way off.

I saw no one on the way back. Charlie had gone inside and the car he had been working on was no longer there. I drank water from the kitchen tap. I read somewhere that a glass of water from a London tap has been drunk five times before. It tasted metallic. It reminded me of the stainless steel table they put the little girl on, her corpse. They probably use tap water to clean the mortuary table tops. I was due to meet the girl's parents at 7 p.m. It was not my idea, it was the idea of one of the police sergeants, the one who took my statement. I should have been firm, but he got round me, he frightened me. When he spoke he held me by the elbow. It could be a trick they learn at police school to give them the power they need. He caught me as I was leaving the building and steered me into a corner. I could not shake him off without wrestling with him. He spoke kindly, urgently, in a cracked whisper. 'You were the last one to see the little girl before she died ...' He lingered over this last word. '... And the parents, you know, of course they'd like to meet you.' He frightened me with his implications, whatever they were, and while he touched me he had the power. He tightened his hold a little. 'So I said you'd be along. You're almost next door to them, aren't you?' I think I looked away and nodded. He smiled, and it was fixed. Still, it was something, a meeting, an event to make sense of the day. In the late afternoon I decided to take a bath and dress up. I had time to kill. I found a bottle of cologne I had never opened before, and a clean shirt. While the bath ran I took off my clothes and stared at my body in the mirror. I am a suspicious-looking person, I know, because I have no chin. Although they could not say why, they suspected me at the police station before I even made a statement. I told them I was standing on the bridge and that I saw her from the bridge, running along the canal. The police sergeant said,

'That was quite a coincidence, then, wasn't it? I mean, her living in the same street as you.' My chin and my neck are the same thing, and it breeds distrust. My mother's was like that, too. Only after I had left home did I find her grotesque. She died last year. Women do not like my chin, they won't come near me. It was the same for my mother, she never had friends. She went everywhere alone, even on holidays. Each year she went to Littlehampton and sat in a deck-chair by herself, facing out to sea. Towards the end of her life she became vicious and thin, like a whippet.

Until last Thursday when I saw Jane's corpse I never had special thoughts about death. I saw a dog run over once. I saw the wheel go over its neck and its eyeballs burst. It meant nothing to me at the time. And when my mother died I stayed away, from indifference, mainly, and a distaste for my relatives. I had no curiosity either about seeing her dead, thin and grey among the flowers. I imagine my own death to be something like hers. But at that time I had not seen a corpse. A corpse makes you compare living with dead. They led me down a stone staircase and along a corridor. I thought the mortuary would stand by itself, but it was in an office building, seven storeys high. We were in the basement. I heard typewriters from the foot of the stairs. The sergeant was there, and a couple of others in suits. He held the swing doors open for me. I did not really think she was going to be there. I forget now what I was expecting, a photograph, perhaps, and some documents to sign. I had not thought the matter out. But she was there. There were five high stainless-steel tables in a row. And there were fluorescent lights in green tin hoods hanging on long chains from the ceiling.

She was on the table nearest the door. She was on her back, palms turned upwards, legs together, mouth wide open, eyes wide open, very pale, very quiet. Her hair was still a little damp. Her red dress looked newly washed. She smelled faintly of the canal. I suppose it was nothing exceptional if you had seen enough corpses, like the police sergeant. There was a small bruise over her right eye. I wanted to touch her but I had the feeling they were watching me closely. Like a secondhand-car salesman, the man in the white coat said briskly,

'Only nine years old.' No one responded, we all looked at her face. The sergeant came round my side of the table with some papers in his hand.

'O.K.?' he said. We went back down the long corridor. Upstairs I signed the papers which said that I had been walking across the footbridge by the railway lines and that I had seen a girl, identified as the one downstairs, running along the canal towpath. I looked away and a little later I saw something red in the water which sank out of sight. Since I cannot swim I fetched a policeman, who peered into the water and said he could see nothing. I gave my name and address and went home. An hour and a half later they pulled her up from the bottom with a dragline. I signed three copies of the statement. After that I did not leave the building for a long time. In one of the corridors I found a moulded plastic chair and sat in it. Opposite me, through an open doorway, I could see two girls typing in their office. They saw me watching them and spoke to each other and laughed. One of them came out smiling and asked me if I was being seen to. I told her I was just sitting and thinking. The girl went back into her office, leaned across her desk and told her friend. They glanced at me uneasily. They suspected me of something, they always do. I was not really thinking about the dead girl downstairs. I had confused images of her, alive and dead, but I tried not to reconcile them. I sat there all afternoon because I did not feel like going anywhere else. The girls closed their office door. I finally left because everyone had gone home and they wanted to lock up. I was the last to leave the building.

I took a long time getting dressed. I ironed my black suit, I thought black was appropriate. I chose a blue tie because I did not want to go too far with the black. Then, as I was about to leave the house, I changed my mind. I went back upstairs and took off the suit, shirt and tie. I was suddenly annoyed at myself for my preparations. Why was I so anxious to have their approval? I put on the old trousers and sweater I was wearing before. I regretted taking a bath and I tried to wash the cologne off the back of my neck. But there was another smell, that of the scented soap I had used in the bath. I used the same soap on Thursday, and that was the first thing the little girl said to me,

'You smell like flowers.' I was walking past her small front garden, setting off on a walk. I ignored her. I avoid talking to children, I find it hard to get the right tone with them. And their directness bothers me, it cramps me. I had seen this one many times before playing in the street, usually by herself, or watching Charlie. She came out of her garden and followed me.

'Where are you going?' she said. Again I ignored her, hoping she would lose interest in me. Furthermore, I had no clear idea where I was walking to. She asked me again, 'Where are you going?'

After a pause I said, 'Never you mind.' She walked right behind me where I could not see her. I had the feeling she was imitating my walk but I did not turn round to look.

'Are you going to Mr Watson's shop?'

'Yes I'm going to Mr Watson's shop.'

She came up level with me. 'Because it's closed today,' she said, 'it's Wednesday.' I had no reply to this. When we came to the corner at the end of the street she said,

'Where are you going really?' I looked at her closely for the first time. She had a long delicate face and large mournful eyes. Her fine brown hair was tied in bunches in red ribbon to match her red cotton dress. She was beautiful in a strange almost sinister way, like a girl in a Modigliani painting. I said,

'I don't know, I'm just going for a walk.'

'I want to come.' I said nothing, and we walked together towards the shopping centre. She was silent too, and walked a little behind me as if she was waiting for me to tell her to turn back. She brought out a game which all the children have round here. They have two hard balls on the ends of pieces of string which they knock together rapidly by some motion of their hand. It makes a clacking sound like a football rattle. I think she was doing it to please me. It made it harder to send her away. And I had spoken to no one in several days.

When I came downstairs after changing my clothes again it was a quarter past six. Jane's parents lived twelve houses away on my side of the street. Since I had finished my preparations forty-five minutes early, I decided on a walk to kill time. The street was in shadow now. I hesitated by the front door, thinking of the best route. Charlie was across the road repairing another car. He saw me, and without particularly wanting to I walked over to him. He looked up without smiling.

'Where you off to this time?' He spoke to me as if I were a child.

'Taking some air,' I said, 'taking some evening air.'

Charlie likes to know what is happening in the street. He knows everyone along here, including all the children. I had often seen the little girl out there with him. The last time she was holding a spanner for him. For some reason Charlie held her death against me. He had had all Sunday to think about it. He wanted to hear my story, but he could not bring himself to ask direct questions.

'Seeing her parents, then? Seven o'clock?'

'Yes, seven o'clock.' He waited for me to go on. I circled round the car. It was large, old and rusty, a Ford Zodiac, the kind of car you get in this street. It belonged to the Pakistani family who ran the small shop at the end of the street. For their own reasons they called the shop 'Watson's'. Their two sons were beaten up by local skinheads. They were saving money now to return to Peshawar. The old man used to tell me about it when I went to his shop, how he was taking his family home because of violence and bad weather in London. Charlie said to me from the other side of Mr Watson's car,

'She was their only.' He was accusing me.

'Yes,' I said, 'I know. Great shame.' We circled round the car. Then Charlie said,

'It was in the paper. Did you see it? It said you saw her go down.'

'That's right.'

'Couldn't reach her, then?'

'No, I couldn't. She sank.' I made my circle round the car wider and edged off. I knew Charlie's eyes were on me all the way down the street, but I did not turn round to acknowledge his suspicion.

At the end of the street I pretended to look up at an aeroplane and glanced back over my shoulder. Charlie was standing by the car, hands on hips, still watching me. There was a large black-and-white cat sitting at his feet.

I saw all this in a glimpse and turned the corner. It was half past six. I decided to walk to the library to use up the remaining time. It was the same walk I took earlier on. There were more people about now. I passed a group of West Indian boys playing football in the street. Their ball rolled towards me and I stepped over it. They stood about waiting while one of the younger boys collected the ball. As I edged past them they were silent, and watching me closely. As soon as I was past, one of them threw a small stone along the road at my feet. Without turning and almost without looking I trapped it neatly with my foot. It was an accident I did it so well. They all laughed at this and clapped and cheered me, so that for one elated moment I thought I could go back and join in their game. The ball was returned and they started to play again. The moment passed and I walked on. My heart was beating fast from the excitement of it. Even when I came to the library and sat down on the steps I could feel the thumping of my pulse in my temples. Such opportunities are rare for me. I do not meet many people, in fact the only ones I talk to are Charlie and Mr Watson. I speak to Charlie because he is there when I leave my front door; he is always the one to speak first, and there is no avoiding him if I want to leave the house. I do not talk to Mr Watson so much as listen, and I listen because I have to go into his shop to buy groceries. To have someone walking along with me on Wednesday was something of an opportunity, too, even if it was only a little girl with nothing to do. Although I would not have admitted it at the time, I felt pleased that she was genuinely curious about me, and I was attracted to her. I wanted her to be my friend.

But I was uneasy at first. She was walking a little behind me, playing with her toy and, for all I knew, making gestures behind my back the way children do. Then, when we came to the main shopping street, she came up to my side.

'Why don't you go to work?' she said. 'My dad goes to work every day except Sunday.'

'I don't need to go to work.'

'Have you got lots of money already?' I nodded. 'Really lots?'

'Yes.'

'Could you buy me something if you wanted to?'

'If I wanted to.' She was pointing at a toyshop window.

'One of those, please, go on, one of those, go on.' She was hanging on my arm, she was making a greedy little dance on the pavement and trying to push me towards the shop. No one had touched me intentionally like that for a long time, not since I was a child. I felt a cold thrill in my stomach and I was unsteady on my legs. I had some money in my pocket and I could see no reason why I should not buy her something. I made her wait outside while I went in the shop and bought her what she wanted, a small, pink, naked doll, moulded from one piece of plastic. Once she had it she seemed to lose interest in it. Farther down the same street she asked me to buy her an ice cream. She stood in the doorway of the shop waiting for me to follow. She did not touch me this time. Of course, I hesitated, I was not sure what was happening. But I was curious about her now, and the effect she was having on me. I gave her enough money to buy ices for both of us and let her go in and get them. She was obviously used to gifts. When we were a little farther down the street I asked her in the friendliest way,

'Don't you say thank you when someone gives you things?' She looked at me scornfully, her thin, pale lips circled with ice cream:

'No.'

I asked her her name. I wanted our conversation to be amiable.

'Jane.'

'What happened to the doll I bought you, Jane?' She glanced down at her hand.

'I left it in the sweet shop.'

'Didn't you want it?'

'I forgot it.' I was about to tell her to run back and get it when I realized how much I wanted her to stay with me, and how close we were to the canal.

The canal is the only stretch of water near here. There is something special about walking by water, even brown stinking water running along the backs of factories. Most of the factories overlooking the canal are windowless and deserted. You can walk a mile and a half along the tow-path and usually you meet no one. The path goes by an old scrap yard. Up until two years ago a quiet old man watched over the pile of junk from a small tin hut outside which, chained to a post, he kept a large Alsatian dog. It was too old to bark. Then the hut, the old man and the dog disappeared and the gate was padlocked. Gradually the surrounding fence was trampled down by the local kids, so that now only the gate stands. The scrap yard is the only thing of interest in that mile and a half because for the rest of the walk the path runs close to the factory walls. But I like the canal and I find it less of a confinement there by the water than anywhere else in this part of town. After walking with me in silence for a while Jane asked me again,

'Where are you going? Where are you going to walk?'

'Along the canal.'

She thought about this for a minute. 'I'm not allowed by the canal.'

'Why not?'

'Because.' She was walking slightly in front of me now. The white ring around her mouth had dried. My legs were weak and I felt suffocated by the sun's heat rising off the pavement. It had become a necessity to persuade her to walk along the canal with me. I sickened at the idea. I threw the rest of my ice cream away, and said,

'I walk along the canal nearly every day.'

'Why?'

'It's very peaceful there ... and there are all kinds of things to look at.'

'What things?'

'Butterflies.' The word was out before I could retrieve it. She turned round to me, suddenly interested. Butterflies could never survive near the canal, the stench would dissolve them. It would not take her long to find that out.

'What colour butterflies?'

'Red ones ... yellow ones.'

'What else is there?'

I hesitated. 'There's a scrap yard.' She wrinkled her nose. I continued quickly, 'And boats, too, boats on the canal.'

'Real boats?'

'Yes, of course, real boats.' Again this was not what I had intended. She stopped walking and I stopped too. She said,

'You won't tell on me if I come, will you?'

'No, I won't tell anyone, but you have to keep close to me when we're walking along the canal, understand?' She nodded. 'And wipe the ice cream off your mouth.' She trailed the back of her hand vaguely across her face. 'Come here, let me do it.' I pulled her towards me and cupped my left hand round the back of her neck. I wetted the forefinger of the other hand, the way I had seen parents do it, and ran it round her lips. I had never touched another person's lips before, nor had I experienced this kind of pleasure. It rose painfully from my groin to my chest and lodged itself there, like a fist pushing against my ribs. I wetted the same finger again and tasted the sticky sweetness on the end of it. I rubbed it round her lips once more and this time she pulled away.

'You hurt me,' she said. 'You pressed too hard.' We walked on, and now she kept close by me.

To get down to the towpath we had to cross the canal first by a narrow black bridge with high walls. Half way across, Jane stood on tiptoe and tried to look over the wall.

'Lift me up,' she said, 'I want to look at the boats.'

'You can't see them from here.' But I placed my hands round her waist and lifted her up. Her short red dress rode up over her backside and I felt the fist in my chest again. She called over her shoulder to me,

'The river's very dirty.'

'It's always been dirty,' I said, 'it's a canal.' As we walked down the stone steps to the towpath Jane moved closer to me. I had the feeling she was holding her breath. Usually the canal flows north, but today it was completely still. On the surface there were patches of yellow scum, and they did not move either because there was no wind to push them along. Occasionally a car passed on the bridge above us and beyond that there was the distant sound of London traffic. Apart from that it was very quiet by the canal. Because of the heat the canal smell was stronger today, an animal rather than a chemical smell given off by the scum. Jane whispered,

'Where are the butterflies?'

'They're not far. We have to go under two bridges first.'

'I want to go back. I want to go back.' We were now

over a hundred yards from the stone steps. She wanted to stop but I was urging her along. She was too frightened to leave my side and run back to the steps by herself.

'Not far now and we'll see the butterflies. Red ones, yellow ones, sometimes green ones.' I abandoned myself to the lie, I did not care what I told her now. She put her hand in mine.

'And what about the boats?'

'You'll see them. Farther up.' We walked on and I thought of nothing but of how to keep her with me. At certain points along the canal there are tunnels under factories, roads and railway lines. The first of these we came to was formed by a three-storey building which connects the factories on either side of the canal. It was empty now, like all the factories, and all the nearer windows were broken. At the entrance to this tunnel Jane tried to pull back.

'What's that noise? Let's not go in there.' She could hear water dripping from the roof of the tunnel into the canal, it echoed in a strange, hollow way.

'It's only water,' I said. 'Look, you can see through to the other side.' The path was very narrow in the tunnel so I made her walk in front of me and kept my hand on her shoulder. She was shivering. At the far end she stopped suddenly and pointed. Where the sunlight entered the tunnel a little way there was a flower growing from between the bricks. It looked like some kind of dandelion, growing out of a small tuft of grass.

'It's coltsfoot,' she said, and picked it and put it in her hair, behind her ear. I said,

'I've never seen flowers along here before.'

'There have to be flowers,' she explained, 'for the butterflies.'

For the next quarter of an hour we walked in silence.

Jane spoke once to ask me again about the butterflies. She seemed less afraid of the canal now and let go of my hand. I wanted to touch her but I could think of no way of doing that without frightening her. I tried to think of a conversation we might have but my mind was blank. The path was beginning to widen out to our right. Round the next bend of the canal in an immense space between a factory and a warehouse was the scrap yard. There was black smoke in the sky ahead of us, and as we came round the bend I saw that it was coming from the scrap yard. A group of boys stood round the fire they had built. They were some kind of gang, they all wore the same blue jackets and cropped hair. As far as I could tell they were preparing to roast a live cat. The smoke hung above them in the still air, behind them the scrapheap towered like a mountain. They had the cat tied up by its neck to a post, the same post the Alsatian dog used to be tied to. The cat's front and back legs were tied together. They were con- structing a cage over the fire made up of pieces of wire fencing and as we came past one of them was dragging the cat by the string around its neck towards the fire. I took Jane's hand and walked faster. They were working intently and in silence, and they hardly paused to glance up at us. Jane kept her eyes on the ground. Through her hand I could feel her whole body shaking.

'What were they doing to that cat?'

'I don't know.' I looked back over my shoulder. It was difficult to see what they were doing now because of the black smoke. We were leaving them far behind and our path was once more along the factory walls. Jane was almost crying, and her hand was only in mine because I I was holding it hard. It was not necessary really for there was nowhere she would dare run by herself. Back along the path past the scrap yard, or forwards into the tunnel we were approaching. I had no idea what was going to happen when we came to the end of the path. She would want to run home, and I just knew I could not let her go. I put it out of my mind. At the entrance to the second tunnel, Jane stopped.

'There aren't any butterflies, are there?' Her voice rose at the end because she was about to cry. I started to tell her that perhaps it was too hot for them. But she was not listening to me, she was wailing,

'You said a lie, there aren't any butterflies, you said a lie.' She started to cry in a half-hearted, miserable way and tried to pull her hand free from mine. I reasoned with her but she would not listen. I tightened my grip on her hand and pulled her into the tunnel. She was screaming now, a piercing continuous sound echoing back from the walls and roof of the tunnel and filling my head. I carried and dragged her right into the tunnel, about half way. And there, suddenly, her screams were drowned out by the thunder of a train going over our heads, and the air and the ground shook together. It took a long time for the train to pass. I held her arms at her sides, but she did not struggle, the din was overpowering her. When the last echoes had died away she said dully,

'I want my mummy.' I unzipped my fly. I did not know if she could see in the dark what was stretching out towards her.

'Touch it,' I said, and shook her gently by the shoulder. She did not move, so I shook her again.

'Touch me, go on. You know what I mean, don't you?' It was quite a simple thing I wanted really. This time I took her in both hands and shook her hard and shouted.

'Touch it, touch it.' She reached out her hand and her fingers briefly brushed my tip. It was enough, though. I doubled up and came, I came into my cupped hands. Like the train, it took a long time, pumping it all out into my hand. All the time I spent by myself came pumping out, all the hours walking alone and all the thoughts I had had, it all came out into my hand. When it was over I remained in that position for several minutes, bent up with my cupped hands in front of me. My mind was clear, my body was relaxed and I was thinking of nothing. I lay on my stomach, reached down and washed my hands in the canal. It was difficult to get the stuff off in cold water. It stuck to my fingers like scum. I picked it off in bits. Then I remembered the girl, she was no longer with me. I could not let her run home now, not after this. I would have to go after her. I stood and saw her silhouetted against the end of the tunnel. She was walking slowly along the edge of the canal in a daze. I could not run quickly because I could not see the ground in front of me. The nearer I got to the sunlight at the end of the tunnel, the harder it was to see. Jane was almost out of the tunnel. When she heard my footsteps behind her she turned round and gave a kind of yelp. She started to run too, and immediately lost her footing. From where I was it was difficult to see what happened to her, her silhouette against the sky suddenly disappeared into the black. She was lying face down when I reached her, with her left leg trailing off the path almost into the water. She had banged her head going down and there was a swelling over her right eye. Her right arm was stretched out in front of her and almost reached into the sunlight. I bent down to her face and listened to her breathing. It was deep and regular. Her eyes were closed tight and the lashes were still wet from crying. I no longer wanted to touch her, that was all pumped out of me now, into the canal. I brushed away some dirt from her face and some more from the back of her red dress.

'Silly girl,' I said, 'no butterflies.' Then I lifted her up gently, as gently as I could so as not to wake her, and eased her quietly into the canal.

I usually sit by the library steps, I prefer it to going inside and reading books. There is more to learn outside. I sat there now, Sunday evening, listening to my pulse slow down to its daily rhythm. Over and over again I ran through what had happened, and what I should have done. I saw the stone skimming along the road, and I saw myself trap it neatly with my foot, almost without turning. I should have turned round then, slowly, acknowledging their applause with a faint grin. Then I should have kicked the stone back, or better, stepped over it and walked casually towards them, and then, when the ball came back, I would be with them, one of them, in a team. I would play with them out there in the street most evenings, learn all their names and they would know mine. I would see them in town during the day and they would call out to me from the other side of the street, cross over and chat. At the end of the game one of them comes over to me and grips my arm.

'See you tomorrow, then ...'

'Yes, tomorrow.' We would go out drinking together when they were older, and I would learn to like beer. I stood up and began to walk slowly back the way I had come. I knew I would not be joining any football games. The opportunities are rare, like butterflies. You stretch your hand out and they are gone. I went along the street where they had been playing. It was deserted now and the stone I had stopped with my foot was still in the middle of the road. I picked it up and put it in my pocket, and then walked on to keep my appointment.

Conversation

with a Cupboard Man

You ask me what I did when I saw this girl. Well, I'll tell you. You see that cupboard there, it takes up most of the room. I ran all the way back here, climbed inside and tossed myself off. Don't think I thought about the girl while I did it. No, I couldn't bear that. I went back in my mind till I was three feet high. That made it come quicker. I can see you think I'm dirty and bent. Well, I washed my hands afterwards, which is more than some people. And I felt better too. Do you see what I mean, I unwound. The way things have been up here in this room what else is there? It's all right for you. I bet you live in a clean house and your wife washes the sheets and the government pays you to find out about people. All right, I know you're a … what is it? … a social worker and you're trying to help, but you can do me no good except by listening. I won't change now, I've been me too long. But it's good to talk so I'll just tell you about myself.

I never saw my father because he died before I was born. I think problems started right there – it was my mother who brought me up and no one else. We lived in a huge house near Staines. She was twisted up, you know, that's where I got it from. All she wanted was to have children but she wouldn't think of getting married again so that left only me; I had to be all the children she had ever wanted. She tried to stop me growing up and for a long time she succeeded. Do you know, I didn't learn to speak properly till I was eighteen. I got no schooling, she kept me home because she said it was a rough area. She had her arms round me day and night. She didn't like it when I got too big for my cot so she went out and bought a crib bed from a hospital auction. That was the sort of thing she would do. Right up until I left I was still sleeping in that thing. I couldn't go to sleep in an ordinary bed, I thought I was going to fall out and I could never get to sleep. When I was two inches taller than her she was still trying to tie a bib round my neck. She was insane. She got a hammer and nails and some pieces of wood and tried to make a kind of high chair for me to sit in, and that was when I was fourteen. Well, you can imagine, the thing just fell to bits as soon as I sat in it. But Christ! The mush she used to feed me on. That's why I get these stomach troubles. She wouldn't let me do anything for myself, even tried to stop me from being clean. I could hardly move without her, and she loved it, the bitch.

Why didn't I run off then when I was older? You might think there was nothing to stop me. But listen, it never occurred to me. I didn't know any other life, I didn't think I was different. Anyway, how could I run away when I would be shitting myself with terror before I got fifty yards down the street? And where'd I go? I could hardly tie my own shoelaces, let alone get a job. Do I sound bitter about it now? I'll tell you a funny thing. I wasn't unhappy, you know. She was all right really. She used to read me stories and that, and we used to make things out of cardboard. We had a kind of theatre we made ourselves out of a fruit box, and we made the people out of paper and card. No, I wasn't unhappy till I found out what other people thought about me. I suppose I could have spent the whole of my life living my first two years over and over again and still not think I was unhappy. She was a good woman really, my mother. Just twisted, that's all.

How did I become an adult? I'll tell you, I never did learn. I have to pretend. All the things you take for granted I have to do it all consciously. I'm always thinking about it, like I was on the stage. I'm sitting in this chair with my arms folded, that's all right, but I'd rather be lying on the floor gurgling to myself than be talking to you. I can see you think I'm joking. It still takes me a long time to get dressed in the morning, and lately I haven't bothered anyway. And you've seen how clumsy I am with a knife and fork. I'd rather someone came and patted me on the back and fed me with a spoon. Do you believe me? Do you think it's disgusting? Well, I do. It's the most disgusting thing I know. That's why I spit on the memory of my mother because she made me this way.

I'll tell you how I came to learn to pretend to be an adult. When I was seventeen my mother was just thirty-eight. She was still an attractive woman and looked much younger. If it wasn't for her obsession with me she could have got married as easy as that. But she was too busy trying to push me back up her womb to think of things like that. That was until she met this bloke, and then it all changed, just like that. Overnight she just swapped obsessions and all the sex she'd missed out on caught up with her. She went mad for this fellow, as if she wasn't mad enough already. She wanted to bring him home but she didn't dare in case he saw me, a seventeen-year-old baby. That's why in two months I had a lifetime's growing up to do. She started hitting me when I spilt food or pronounced words wrongly or even when I was just standing there watching her doing something. And then she started going out in the evenings, leaving me alone in the house. This intensive training really threw me. To have someone all over you for seventeen years and then find yourself at war. I started getting these headaches. And then the fits, especially when she was getting ready to go out in the evenings. My arms and legs would go right out of control, my tongue did things by itself as if it belonged to someone else. It was a nightmare. Then everything went as black as hell. When I came round my mother would have gone out anyway and I'd be lying there in my own shit in that dark house. It was a bad time.

I think the fits became less frequent because one day she brought her man home. I was fairly presentable by that time. My mother passed me off as mentally subnormal, which I suppose I was. I can't remember much about the bloke except that he was very large with long hair greased back. He always wore blue suits. He owned a garage in Clapham and because he was big and successful he hated me at first sight. You can imagine how I looked then, I had hardly been out of the house in my life. I was thin and bloodless, even thinner and weaker than I am now. I hated him too because he had taken my mother. First time he just nodded when my mother introduced me to him and after that he never said a word to me. He didn't even notice me. He was so big and strong and full of himself I suppose he couldn't bear to think that people like me existed.

He came to our house pretty regularly, usually to take my mother out somewhere for the evening. I watched the telly. I got pretty lonely then. When the programmes had finished for the night I used to sit in the kitchen and wait up for my mother, and though I was seventeen I used to cry a lot. One morning I came down and found my mother's boyfriend having his breakfast in his dressing-gown. He didn't even look up at me when I came in the kitchen. When I looked at my mother she just pretended to be busy at the sink. After that his stays became more and more frequent till he was sleeping in our house every night. One afternoon they got dressed up smart and went out. When they came back they were laughing and falling about all over the place. They must have been drinking a lot. That night my mother told me they had got married and that I had to call him Father. That was the end. I had a fit, the worst one ever. I can't explain how bad it really was, it seemed to last for days, though it was only an hour or so. When it finished I opened my eyes and saw the look on my mother's face, complete disgust it was. You've no idea how much a person can change in such a short time. When I saw that look I realized she was as much a stranger to me as my father.

I stayed with them three months before they found a home to put me into. They were too busy with each other to notice me. They hardly spoke to me at all and they never spoke to each other when I was in the room. You know, I was pretty glad to get out of that place, even though it was my home, and I did cry a little when I left. But mostly I was glad to get away from them. And I suppose they were glad to see the last of me. It wasn't bad at the home they took me to. I didn't care where I was really. But they taught me to look after myself better and I even started to learn to read and write, though I've forgotten most of that now. I couldn't read that form you sent me, could I? That was pretty stupid. Anyway, it wasn't a bad life at this place. There were all kinds of weird people there and that made me feel more sure of myself. Three times a week they took me and a few others in a bus to a workshop place where we learned how to repair watches and clocks. The idea was that when I left I would be able to stand by myself and earn a living. I've never earned a penny from it yet. You go for a job and they ask you where you got your training. When you tell them they don't want to know about it. One of the best things about the place was that I met Mr Smith. I know it doesn't sound much of a name, and he looked pretty ordinary so you wouldn't expect him to be anything special. But he was. He was in charge of the home and it was him who tried to teach me to read. I did all right. By the time I left I had just finished reading *The Hobbit* and I enjoyed that. But once I was outside I didn't have much time for that sort of thing. Still, old Smith had a good try at teaching me. And he taught me a lot of other things. I was still slurring my words when I arrived there and he corrected me every time I spoke. Then I had to repeat it the way he said it. And then he used to say I needed more grace. Yes, grace! In his room he had this enormous record player and he would put on records and make me dance. I felt bloody stupid about that at first. He told me to forget where I was and relax my body and drift about to the feel of the music. So I pranced round the room waving my arms and kicking my legs and hoping that no one could see me through the window. And then I started to enjoy it. It was almost like having a fit, you know, except that it was pleasant. I mean I could really lose myself, if you can imagine that. Then the record stopped and I'd be standing there sweating and catching my breath, feeling a bit of a nutter. Old Smith didn't mind, though. I danced for him twice a week, Mondays and Fridays. There were days when he played the piano instead of the records. I didn't enjoy that so much but I never said a word because I could see from his face that he was enjoying it.

And he started me on painting. Not ordinary painting, mind. Say, if you wanted to paint a tree you'd probably make a brown bit down and a green blob on the top. He said this was all wrong. There was a big garden at this place and one morning he took me out by some old trees. We stopped under one of them, a massive one it was. He said he wanted me to ... what was it ... I had to sense the tree and then re-create it. It was a long time before I saw what he was getting at. I went on painting in my own way. Then he showed me what he meant. He said suppose I wanted to paint that oak tree. What did I think of? Bigness, solidness, darkness. He painted thick black lines on the paper. I got the idea then and started painting things the way I felt about them. He told me to paint a picture of myself, and I painted these strange shapes in yellow and white. And after that my mother, and I made large red mouths all over the paper – that was her lipstick – and in the mouths I painted it black. That was because I hated her. Though I didn't really. I've never done any painting since I left, there isn't room for that sort of thing outside a place like that.

If I'm boring you just say so, I know you have to see a lot of people. No reason why you should sit with me. All right then. It was one of the rules of the home that you had to leave when you were twenty-one. I remember they made me a cake by way of compensation, except that I don't like cake so I gave it to the other kids. They gave me letters of introduction and the names and addresses of people to go and see. I didn't want to know about that. I wanted to be on my own. It means a lot when you've had people looking after you all your life, even if they are good to you. So I came to London. I managed it at first, I felt strong in my mind, you know, I felt as though I could take on London. It was all new then and exciting for someone who

had never been there in his life before. I found a room in
Muswell Hill and started looking for a job. The only kind
of jobs I came near to getting were lifting and carrying or
digging. They'd take one look at me and tell me to forget it.
Finally I found a job in a hotel, washing-up. It was a
swanky place – the bit where the guests were, I mean.
Deep red carpets and cut-glass chandeliers and a small
orchestra playing in one corner of the hallway. I walked
in the front bit by mistake on my first day. The kitchen
wasn't so fine. Christ, no, it was a filthy shit-hole. They
must have been understaffed because I was the only one
washing-up. Or perhaps they saw me coming. Whatever
it was, I had to do it all by myself, twelve hours a day with
forty-five minutes for lunch.

I wouldn't have minded the hours of the work, I was
pleased to be earning my own living for the first time in
my life. No, it was the chief cook who really got me. He
paid the wages and he was always cutting me short. The
money of course went straight into his own pocket. He was
an ugly bastard too. You never saw such spots. Over his
face and forehead, under his chin, round by his ears, even
on his ear lobes. Great puffy spots and scabs, red and
yellow ones, I don't know why they let him near the food.
Still, they didn't care too much about that sort of thing in
that kitchen. They would have cooked the cockroaches if
they had known how to catch them. The chief cook really
got me. He used to call me scarecrow, and that was a great
joke. 'Hey Scarecrow! Scared any more birds away?' He
was one to talk. There could be no woman who would go
near all that pus. His head was full of pus because he was a
dirty-minded bastard. Always slobbering over his magazines. He used to chase after the women who were meant
to keep the kitchen clean. They were all hags, none of
them were under sixty, most of them black and ugly. I can

see him now, giggling and spitting and running his hands up their skirts. The women didn't dare say anything because he could throw them out. You might say that at least he was normal. But I'd rather be me any day.

Because I didn't laugh at his jokes like the others, Pus-face started getting really nasty. He went out of his way to find me more work to do, all the dirty jobs were mine. I was getting sick of all the scarecrow jokes, too, so one day when he'd made me scour all the pots three times over I said, 'Fuck off, Pus-face.' That really stung him. No one ever called him that to his face before. He left me alone for the rest of that day. But first thing next morning he came over to me and said, 'Get and clean the main oven.' There was this enormous cast-iron oven, see, and it got cleaned once a year, I think. Its walls were covered with a thick black scum. To get it off you had to get inside with a bowl of water and a scraper. It smelled like rotten cats inside that oven. I got a bowl of water and some scourers and crawled inside. You couldn't breath through your nose or you'd throw up. I had been in there ten minutes when the oven door shut. Pus-face had locked me in. I could just hear him laughing through the iron walls. He kept me in there five hours, till after my lunch break. Five hours in that stinking black oven, and after that he made me do the washing-up. You can imagine how furious I was. I wanted to keep my job so there was nothing I could say.

The very next morning Pus-face came up to me as I was beginning to wash up the breakfast plates. 'I thought I told you to clean that oven, Scarecrow.' So once again I got my things and crawled inside. And as soon as I was in the door slammed. I went mad. I screamed every name I could think of at Pus-face, and I hammered on the walls till my hands were raw. But I couldn't hear anything so

after a while I calmed down and tried to get comfortable.
I had to keep moving my legs so as not to get cramp. After
I had been in there what seemed six hours I heard Pus-face
laughing outside. Then it started to get hot. I couldn't
believe it at first, I thought I was imagining things. Pus-
face had turned on the oven at its lowest marking. It soon
got too hot to sit down and I had to crouch. I could feel
it burning through my shoes, it was burning my face and
up my nostrils. The sweat was running off me and every
mouthful of air scorched my throat. I couldn't bang on the
walls because they were too hot to touch. I wanted to
scream but I couldn't afford the air. I thought I was going
to die because I knew Pus-face was capable of roasting me
alive. In the late afternoon he let me out. I was almost
unconscious but I heard him say, 'Ah, Scarecrow, where've
you been all day? I wanted you to clean out the oven.'
Then he laughed and the others joined in, only because
they were scared of him. I got a taxi home and went to
bed. I was in a real mess. The next morning I was worse.
There were blisters on my feet and down my spine where I
must have leaned against the oven wall. And I was throw-
ing up. There was one thing I was sure of in my mind,
and that was that I had to get to work to even up with
Pus-face, if it meant dying in the attempt. It was torture
to walk so I took another taxi. Somehow I managed to get
through the first part of the morning until break. Pus-face
left me alone. During the break he was sitting by himself
reading one of his dirty magazines. Just before it was time
I lit the gas under one of the chip pans. It held about four
pints and when the oil was boiling I carried it over to
where Pus-face was sitting. The pain in the soles of my
feet made me want to cry out. My heart was thumping
because I knew I was going to get Pus-face. I came up
level with his chair. He glanced up and by the look on my

face he knew exactly what was going to happen to him. But he didn't have time to move. I let the oil fall right into his lap, and for the benefit of anyone watching I pretended to slip. Pus-face howled like a wild animal, I never heard a man make a noise like that. His clothes seemed to dissolve and I could see his balls red and swelling and then turning white. It was all down his legs. He was screaming for twenty-five minutes before the doctor came and gave him morphine. I found out later that Pus-face spent nine months in hospital while they picked out the bits of clothing from his flesh. That was how I sorted Pus-face out.

I was too ill to stay in my job after that. I had paid my rent in advance and saved a little money. The next two weeks I spent hobbling from my room to the doctor's surgery each day. When the blisters had gone I started looking for another job. But by this time I didn't feel so strong. London was becoming too much for me. I found it hard to get out of bed in the mornings. It was better under the bedclothes, I was safer there. I was depressed by the thought of facing thousands of people, thundering traffic, queues and things like that. I began to think back to the old days when I was with my mother. I wished I was back there. The old cotton-wool life when everything was done for me, warm and safe. It sounds pretty stupid, I know, but I started thinking that perhaps my mother had got tired of that man she had married and that if I went back we could carry on the old life. Well, this was on my mind for days until I became obsessed by it. I thought of nothing else. I convinced myself that she was waiting for me, perhaps she had the police out looking for me. I had to go home and then she would take me in her arms, she would feed me with a spoon, we would make another cardboard theatre together. One evening I was thinking of this when I decided to go to her. What was I waiting for? I ran out of doors and all the way down the street. I was almost singing with joy. I caught the train to Staines and I ran from the station to our house. It was going to be all right again. I slowed down when I turned down our road. The downstairs lights were on in the house. I rang the bell. My legs were trembling so much that I had to lean against the wall. The person who came to the door was not my mother. It was a girl, a very pretty girl of about eighteen. I couldn't think what to say. There was a stupid silence while I thought of something. Then she asked me who I was. I told her I used to live in the house and that I was looking for my mother. She said she had been living there with her parents for two years. She went inside to find out if any address had been left. While she was gone I was staring into the hallway. Everything was different. There were large book cases and another wall-paper, and a telephone which we never used to have. I felt really sad that it was changed, I felt cheated. The girl came back to tell me that no addresses had been left be-hind. I said goodnight and walked back down the path-way. I was left out. That house was really my own, and I wanted the girl to ask me inside, in the warm. If only she had put her arms round my neck and said, 'Come and live with us.' It sounds pretty stupid, but that was what I was thinking as I walked back to the station.

So I went back to looking for a job. I think it was the oven that did it. I mean it was the oven that made me think I could go back to Staines as if nothing had happened. I thought about that oven a lot. I made up daydreams about being made to stay inside an oven. That sounds incredible, especially after what I did to Pus-face. It was what I felt, though, and I couldn't help that. The more I thought about it, the more I realized that when I went to clean the oven the second time I was secretly wanting to be shut in. I was sort of hoping it without knowing it, do you see what I mean? I wanted to be frustrated. I wanted to be where I couldn't get out. That was at the bottom of my mind. When I was actually in the oven I was too worried about getting out and too furious with Pus-face to enjoy anything. It was in my mind afterwards, that was all.

I had no luck with finding a job and as my money was running out I started stealing from shops. You might think that was an idiotic thing to do but it was dead easy. And what else could I do? I had to eat. I only took a little from each shop, usually from supermarkets. I wore a long overcoat with large pockets. I stole things like frozen meat and tins of things. I also had to pay the rent so I started taking more valuable things and selling them in secondhand shops. This was working quite nicely for about a month. I had all I wanted, and if I wanted something different all I had to do was put it in my pocket. But then I must have got careless because a store detective caught me stealing a watch from a counter. He didn't stop me there as I was doing it. No, he let me take it and then followed me out into the street. I was at the bus stop when he caught me by the arm and told me to come back to the shop. They got the police in and I had to appear in court. It turned out that they had been watching me for quite a while, so I was up for a number of things. Since I had never done anything before they made me report to a probation officer twice a week. That was lucky. I could have got six months straight away. That's what the police sergeant said.

Being on probation didn't get me food or pay the rent. The officer was all right, I suppose, he did his best. There were so many people on his books that he couldn't remember my name from Monday to Thursday. In all the jobs he tried to get me they wanted someone who could read and write, and any other sort of job needed strength for lifting. Anyway, I didn't really want another job. I didn't want to meet any more people and get called Scarecrow again. So what could I do? I started stealing again. More carefully this time and never twice in the same place. But you know, I got caught almost immediately after about a week. I took an ornamental knife from a department store and because my coat pockets had carried so much they must have worn away. Just as I was going through the door the knife went straight out the bottom of my coat on to the floor. There were three of them on to me before I could even turn. I was back in front of the same magistrate again, and this time I got three months.

Prison's a funny place. Not that it would make you laugh. I thought they would all be tough gangsters in there, you know, hard men. But there were only a few like that. The rest were just cracked, like at the home I went to. It wasn't bad there, nowhere near as bad as I thought it was going to be. My cell wasn't very different from my room in Muswell Hill. In fact from the window there was a much better view from my prison room because I was higher up. There was a bed, table, a small book case and a sink. You could cut pictures out of magazines and stick them on the wall, and I wasn't allowed to do that in my room in Muswell Hill. Nor was I locked up in the cell, except for a couple of hours a day. We could wander about and visit the other cells, but only those on your floor. There was an iron gate which stopped you going up or down the stairs out of hours.

There were some strange types in that prison. There was a bloke who used to climb on his chair during meal time and expose himself. I was pretty shocked when it happened first, but everyone went on eating and talking so I did the same. After a while it didn't bother me at all even though he did it quite regular. It's surprising what you can get used to in time. And then there was Jacko. He walked into my cell on the second morning and introduced himself. He said he was in for fraud and he told me how his father was a horse trainer and they were down on their luck. And on and on, a load of things he told me which I've forgotten. Then he walked out. Next time he came up and introduced himself all over again, as if he'd never seen me before in his life. This time he said he was inside for multiple rape and that he'd never been able to satisfy his sexual appetite. I thought he was having me on because I still believed his first story. He was dead serious, though. He had a different story each time he saw me. He never remembered our last conversation or who he was. I don't think he knew who he was himself. Like he didn't have an identity of his own. One of the others told me that Jacko was knocked over the head during an armed robbery. I don't know if that was true or not. You never know what to believe.

Don't get me wrong. They weren't all like that. There were some good blokes and one of the best was Deafy. No one knew his real name, nor could Deafy tell them because he was deaf and dumb. I think he had been inside nearly all his life. His cell was the most comfortable in the whole prison, he was the only one who was allowed to brew up tea for himself. I often sat in his room. Of course, there was no conversation. We just sat there, sometimes we smiled at each other, nothing else. He would make tea – the best I've ever tasted. Some afternoons I would doze in his armchair while he read one of his war comics from a pile he kept in the corner. When I had something on my mind I used to talk to him about it. He couldn't understand a word but he nodded and smiled or looked sad, whatever he thought was needed from the expression on my face. I think he liked to feel that he was taking part in something. Most of the other prisoners ignored him most of the time. He was popular with the guards and they brought him whatever he wanted. Sometimes we'd have chocolate cake with our tea. He could read and write so he wasn't much worse off than I was.

Those three months were the best since I left home. I made my cell comfortable and I fell into a closed routine. I didn't speak to many people apart from Deafy. I didn't want to, I wanted a life without complications. You might be thinking that what I said about being locked in an oven was the same thing as being locked in a cell. No, it wasn't the pain-pleasure of feeling frustrated. It was a deeper pleasure of feeling safe. In fact I remember now wishing sometimes I had less freedom. I enjoyed the time of day we had to keep to our cells. If they had made us stay in them all day I don't think I would have complained, except that I would not have been able to see Deafy. I never had to plan anything. Each day was like the one before it. I didn't have to worry about meals and rent. Time stood still for me, like floating on a lake. I began to worry about coming out. I went to see the assistant governor and asked him if I could stay in. But he said it cost sixteen pounds a week to keep a man inside, and that there were plenty of others waiting to come in. They didn't have room for us all.

I had to come out then. They found me a job in a factory. I moved into this attic room where I've been ever since. In the factory I had to take tins of raspberries off a conveyor belt. I didn't mind that since it was so noisy you didn't have to speak to anyone. Now I'm strange. Not strange to me because I knew it was going to turn out like this. Ever since that oven, I want to be contained. I want to be small. I don't want this noise and these people all

around me. I want to be out of all that, in the dark. Do
you see that wardrobe there, takes up most of this room?
If you look inside you won't find any clothes hanging up.
It's full of cushions and blankets. I go in there, I lock the
door behind me and sit in the darkness for hours. That
must sound pretty stupid to you. I feel all right in there.
I don't get bored or anything, I just sit. Sometimes I wish
the wardrobe would get up and walk around and forget
that I was in there. At first I went in there only very occasionally but then it got more and more frequent till I
started spending whole nights in there. I did not want to
come out in the mornings either so I was late for work.
Then I stopped going to work altogether. It's three months
since I've been. I hate going outside. I prefer it in my
cupboard.

I don't want to be free. That's why I envy these babies
I see in the street being bundled and carried about by their
mothers. I want to be one of them. Why can't it be me?
Why do I have to walk around, go to work, cook my meals
and do all the hundred things you have to do each day to
keep alive? I want to climb in the pram. It's stupid, I'm
six feet tall. But that doesn't make any difference to the
way I feel. The other day I stole a blanket from a pram. I
don't know why, I suppose I had to make contact with
their world, to feel I was not completely irrelevant to it.
I feel excluded. I don't need sex or anything like that. If I
see a pretty girl like the one I was telling you about I get
all bent up inside, and then I come back here and toss
myself off, like I told you. There can't be many like me. I
keep that blanket I stole in the cupboard. I want to fill it
with dozens like it.

I don't go out much now. It's two weeks since I've been
out of this attic. I bought some tins of food last time,
though I am never very hungry. Mostly I sit in the

cupboard thinking about the old times in Staines, wishing it all again. When it rains at night it beats against the roof and I wake up. I think about that girl who lives in our house now, I can hear the wind and the traffic. I want to be one year old again. But it won't happen. I know it won't.

First Love, Last Rites

From the beginning of summer until it seemed pointless, we lifted the thin mattress on to the heavy oak table and made love in front of the large open window. We always had a breeze blowing into the room and smells of the quayside four floors down. I was drawn into fantasies against my will, fantasies of the creature, and afterwards when we lay on our backs on the huge table, in those deep silences I heard it faintly running and clawing. It was new to me, all this, and I worried, I tried to talk to Sissel about it for reassurance. She had nothing to say, she did not make abstractions or discuss situations, she lived inside them. We watched the seagulls wheeling about in our square of sky and wondered if they had been watching us up there, that was the kind of thing we talked about, mildly entertaining hypotheses of the present moment. Sissel did things as they came to her, stirred her coffee, made love, listened to her records, looked out the window. She did not say things like I'm happy, or confused, or I want to make love, or I don't, or I'm tired of the fights in my family, she had no language to split herself in two, so I suffered alone what seemed like crimes in my head while we fucked, and afterwards listened alone to it scrabbling in the silence. Then one afternoon Sissel woke from a doze, raised her head from the mattress and said, 'What's that scratching noise behind the wall?'

My friends were far away in London, they sent me anguished and reflective letters, what would they do now? Who were they, and what was the point of it all? They were my age, seventeen and eighteen, but I pretended not to understand them. I sent back postcards, find a big table and an open window, I told them. I was happy and it seemed easy, I was making eel traps, it was so easy to have a purpose. The summer went on and I no longer heard from them. Only Adrian came to see us, he was Sissel's ten-year-old brother and he came to escape the misery of his disintegrating home, the quick reversals of his mother's moods, the endless competitive piano playing of his sisters, the occasional bitter visits of his father. Adrian and Sissel's parents after twenty-seven years of marriage and six children hated each other with sour resignation, they could no longer bear to live in the same house. The father moved out to a hostel a few streets away to be near his children. He was a businessman who was out of work and looked like Gregory Peck, he was an optimist and had a hundred schemes to make money in an interesting way. I used to meet him in the pub. He did not want to talk about his redundancy or his marriage, he did not mind me living in a room over the quayside with his daughter. Instead he told me about his time in the Korean war, and when he was an international sales-man, and of the legal fraudery of his friends who were now at the top and knighted, and then one day of the eels in the River Ouse, how the river bed swarmed with eels, how there was money to be made catching them and taking them live to London. I told him how I had eighty pounds in the bank, and the next morning we bought netting, twine, wire hoops and an old cistern tank to keep eels in. I spent the next two months making eel traps.

On fine days I took my net, hoops and twine outside and worked on the quay, sitting on a bollard. An eel trap is cylinder-shaped, sealed at one end, and at the other is a long tapering funnel entrance. It lies on the river bed, the eels swim in to eat the bait and in their blindness cannot find their way out. The fishermen were friendly and amused. There's eels down there, they said, and you'll catch a few but you won't make no living on it. The tide'll lose your nets fast as you make them. We're using iron weights, I told them, and they shrugged in a good-natured way and showed me a better way to lash the net to the hoops, they believed it was my right to try it for myself. When the fishermen were out in their boats and I did not feel like working I sat about and watched the tidal water slip across the mud, I felt no urgency about the eel traps but I was certain we would be rich.

I tried to interest Sissel in the eel adventure, I told her about the rowing-boat someone was lending to us for the summer, but she had nothing to say. So instead we lifted the mattress on to the table and lay down with our clothes on. Then she began to talk. We pressed our palms together, she made a careful examination of the size and shape of our hands and gave a running commentary. Exactly the same size, your fingers are thicker, you've got this extra bit here. She measured my eyelashes with the end of her thumb and wished hers were as long, she told me about the dog she had when she was small, it had long white eyelashes. She looked at the sunburn on my nose and talked about that, which of her brothers and sisters went red in the sun, who went brown, what her youngest sister said once. We slowly undressed. She kicked off her plimsolls and talked about her foot rot. I listened with my eyes closed, I could smell mud and seaweed and dust through the open window. Wittering on, she called it, this kind of talk. Then once I was inside her I was moved, I was inside my fantasy, there could be no separation now of my mushrooming sensations from my knowledge that we could make a creature grow in Sissel's belly. I had no wish to be a father, that was not in it at all. It was eggs, sperms, chromosomes, feathers, gills, claws, inches from my cock's end the unstoppable chemistry of a creature growing out of a dark red slime, my fantasy was of being helpless before the age and strength of this process and the thought alone could make me come before I wanted. When I told Sissel she laughed. Oh, Gawd, she said. To me Sissel was right inside the process, she *was* the process and the power of its fascination grew. She was meant to be on the pill and every month she forgot it at least two or three times. Without discussion we came to the arrangement that I was to come outside her, but it rarely worked. As we were swept down the long slopes to our orgasms, in those last desperate seconds I struggled to find my way out but I was caught like an eel in my fantasy of the creature in the dark, waiting, hungry, and I fed it great white gobs. In those careless fractions of a second I abandoned my life to feeding the creature, whatever it was, in or out of the womb, to fucking only Sissel, to feeding more creatures, my whole life given over to this in a moment's weakness. I watched out for Sissel's periods, everything about women was new to me and I could take nothing for granted. We made love in Sissel's copious, effortless periods, got good and sticky and brown with the blood and I thought we were the creatures now in the slime, we were inside fed by gobs of cloud coming through the window, by gases drawn from the mudflats by the sun. I worried about my fantasies, I knew I could not come without them. I asked Sissel what she thought about and she giggled. Not feathers and gills, anyway. What *do* you think about, then? Nothing

much, nothing really. I pressed my question and she withdrew into silence.

I knew it was my own creature I heard scrabbling, and
when Sissel heard it one afternoon and began to worry, I
realized her fantasies were involved too, it was a sound
which grew out of our lovemaking. We heard it when we
were finished and lying quite still on our backs, when we
were empty and clear, perfectly quiet. It was the impression of small claws scratching blindly against a wall, such
a distant sound it needed two people to hear it. We thought
it came from one part of the wall. When I knelt down and
put my ear to the skirting-board it stopped, I sensed it on
the other side of the wall, frozen in its action, waiting in
the dark. As the weeks passed we heard it at other times in
the day, and now and then at night. I wanted to ask Adrian
what he thought it was. Listen, there it is, Adrian, shut
up a moment, what do you think that noise is, Adrian?
He strained impatiently to hear what we could hear
but he would not be still long enough. There's nothing
there, he shouted. Nothing, nothing, nothing. He became very excited, jumped on his sister's back, yelling
and yodelling. He did not want whatever it was to be
heard, he did not want to be left out. I pulled him off
Sissel's back and we rolled about on the bed. Listen again,
I said, pinning him down, there it was again. He struggled
free and ran out of the room shouting his two-tone police-
car siren. We listened to it fade down the stairs and when I
could hear him no more I said, Perhaps Adrian is really
afraid of mice. Rats, you mean, said his sister, and put her
hands between my legs.

By mid-July we were not so happy in our room, there
was a growing dishevelment and unease, and it did not
seem possible to discuss it with Sissel. Adrian was coming
to us every day now because it was the summer holidays

and he could not bear to be at home. We would hear him four floors down, shouting and stamping on the stairs on his way up to us. He came in noisily, doing handstands and showing off to us. Frequently he jumped on Sissel's back to impress me, he was anxious, he was worried we might not find him good company and send him away, send him back home. He was worried too because he could no longer understand his sister. At one time she was always ready for a fight, and she was a good fighter, I heard him boast that to his friends, he was proud of her. Now changes had come over his sister, she pushed him off sulkily, she wanted to be left alone to do nothing, she wanted to listen to records. She was angry when he got his shoes on her skirt, and she had breasts now like his mother, she talked to him now like his mother. Get down off there, Adrian. Please, Adrian, please, not now, later. He could not quite believe it all the same, it was a mood of his sister's, a phase, and he went on taunting and attacking her hopefully, he badly wanted things to stay as they were before his father left home. When he locked his forearms round Sissel's neck and pulled her backwards on to the bed his eyes were on me for encouragement, he thought the real bond was between us, the two men against the girl. He did not see there was no encouragement, he wanted it so badly. Sissel never sent Adrian away, she understood why he was here, but it was hard for her. One long afternoon of torment she left the room almost crying with frustration. Adrian turned to me and raised his eyebrows in mock horror. I tried to talk to him then but he was already making his yodelling sound and squaring up for a fight with me. Nor did Sissel have anything to say to me about her brother, she never made general remarks about people because she never made general remarks. Sometimes when we heard Adrian on his way up the stairs she glanced across at me and seemed to betray herself by a slight pursing of her beautiful lips.

There was only one way to persuade Adrian to leave us in peace. He could not bear to see us touch, it pained him, it genuinely disgusted him. When he saw one of us move across the room to the other he pleaded with us silently, he ran between us, pretending playfulness, wanted to decoy us into another game. He imitated us frantically in a desperate last attempt to show us how fatuous we appeared. Then he could stand it no more, he ran out of the room machine-gunning German soldiers and young lovers on the stairs.

But Sissel and I were touching less and less now, in our quiet ways we could not bring ourselves to it. It was not that we were in decline, not that we did not delight in each other, but that our opportunities were faded. It was the room itself. It was no longer four floors up and detached, there was no breeze through the window, only a mushy heat rising off the quayside and dead jellyfish and clouds of flies, fiery grey flies who found our armpits and bit fiercely, houseflies who hung in clouds over our food. Our hair was too long and dank and hung in our eyes. The food we bought melted and tasted like the river. We no longer lifted the mattress on to the table, the coolest place now was the floor and the floor was covered with greasy sand which would not go away. Sissel grew tired of her records, and her foot rot spread from one foot to the other and added to the smell. Our room stank. We did not talk about leaving because we did not talk about anything. Every night now we were woken by the scrabbling behind the wall, louder now and more insistent. When we made love it listened to us behind the wall. We made love less and our rubbish gathered around us, milk bottles we could not bring ourselves to carry away, grey sweating cheese, butter wrappers, yogurt cartons, over-ripe salami. And among it all Adrian cart-wheeling, yodelling, machine-gunning and attacking Sissel. I tried to write poems about my fantasies, about the creature, but I could see no way in and I wrote nothing down, not even a first line. Instead I took long walks along the river dyke into the Norfolk hinterland of dull beet fields, telegraph poles, uniform grey skies. I had two more eel nets to make, I was forcing myself to sit down to them each day. But in my heart I was sick of them, I could not really believe that eels would ever go inside them and I wondered if I wanted them to, if it was not better that the eels should remain undisturbed in the cool mud at the bottom of the river. But I went on with it because Sissel's father was ready to begin, because I had to expiate all the money and hours I had spent so far, because the idea had its own tired, fragile momentum now and I could no more stop it than carry the milk bottles from our room.

Then Sissel found a job and it made me see we were different from no one, they all had rooms, houses, jobs, careers, that's what they all did, they had cleaner rooms, better jobs, we were anywhere's striving couple. It was one of the windowless factories across the river where they canned vegetables and fruit. For ten hours a day she was to sit in the roar of machines by a moving conveyor belt, talk to no one and pick out the rotten carrots before they were canned. At the end of her first day Sissel came home in a pink-and-white nylon raincoat and pink cap. I said, Why don't you take it off? Sissel shrugged. It was all the same to her, sitting around in the room, sitting around in a factory where they relayed Radio One through speakers strung along the steel girders, where four hundred women half listened, half dreamed, while their hands spun backwards and forwards like powered shuttles. On Sissel's

second day I took the ferry across the river and waited for
her at the factory gates. A few women stepped through a
small tin door in a great windowless wall and a wailing
siren sounded all across the factory complex. Other small
doors opened and they streamed out, converging on the
gates, scores of women in pink-and-white nylon coats and
pink caps. I stood on a low wall and tried to see Sissel, it
was suddenly very important. I thought that if I could not
pick her out from this rustling stream of pink nylon then
she was lost, we were both lost and our time was worthless.
As it approached the factory gates the main body was
moving fast. Some were half running in the splayed, hopeless way that women have been taught to run, the others
walked as fast as they could. I found out later they were
hurrying home to cook suppers for their families, to make
an early start on the housework. Latecomers on the next
shift tried to push their way through in the opposite direction. I could not see Sissel and I felt on the edge of panic,
I shouted her name and my words were trampled under-
foot. Two older women who stopped by the wall to light
cigarettes grinned up at me. Sizzle yerself. I walked home
by the long way, over the bridge, and decided not to tell
Sissel I had been to wait for her because I would have to
explain my panic and I did not know how. She was sitting
on the bed when I came in, she was still wearing her nylon
coat. The cap was on the floor. Why don't you take that
thing off? I said. She said, Was that you outside the
factory? I nodded. Why didn't you speak to me if you saw
me standing there? Sissel turned and lay face downwards
on the bed. Her coat was stained and smelled of machine
oil and earth. I dunno, she said into the pillow, I didn't
think. I didn't think of anything after my shift. Her words
had a deadening finality, I glanced around our room and
fell silent.

Two days later, on Saturday afternoon, I bought pounds of rubbery cows' lungs sodden with blood (lights, they were called) for bait. That same afternoon we filled the traps and rowed out into mid-channel at low tide to lay them on the river bed. Each of the seven traps was marked by a buoy. Four o'clock Sunday morning Sissel's father called for me and we set out in his van to where we kept the borrowed boat. We were rowing out now to find the marker buoys and pull the traps in, it was the testing time, would there be eels in the nets, would it be profitable to make more nets, catch more eels and drive them once a week to Billingsgate market, would we be rich? It was a dull windy morning, I felt no anticipation, only tiredness and a continuous erection. I half dozed in the warmth of the van's heater. I had spent many hours of the night awake listening to the scrabbling noises behind the wall. Once I got out of bed and banged the skirting-board with a spoon. There was a pause, then the digging continued. It seemed certain now that it was digging its way into the room. While Sissel's father rowed I watched over the side for markers. It was not as easy as I thought to find them, they did not show up white against the water but as dark low silhouettes. It was twenty minutes before we found the first. As we pulled it up I was amazed at how soon the clean white rope from the chandlers had become like all other rope near the river, brown and hung about with fine strands of green weed. The net too was old-looking and alien, I could not believe that one of us had made it. Inside were two crabs and a large eel. He untied the closed end of the trap, let the two crabs drop into the water and put the eel in the plastic bucket we had brought with us. We put fresh lights in the trap and dropped it over the side. It took another fifteen minutes to find the next trap and that one had nothing inside. We rowed up and down

San Diego Public Library
DATE DUE SLIP
****

Date due: 3/23/2016,23:59
Title: First love, last rites
Call number: FIC/MCEWAN
Item ID: 31336092709063
Date charged: 3/2/2016,12:43

Date due: 3/23/2016,23:59
Title: The cement garden
Call number: FIC/MCEWAN
Item ID: 31336092709105
Date charged: 3/2/2016,12:43

Total checkouts for session:2
Total checkouts:4

<><><><><><><><><><><>
Renew at
www.sandiegolibrary.org
OR Call 619-236-5800 or
858-484-4440 and press 1
then 2 to RENEW. Your
library card is needed to
renew borrowed items.

the channel for half an hour after that without finding
another trap, and by this time the tide was coming up and
covering the markers. It was then that I took the oars and
made for the shore.

We went back to the hostel where Sissel's father was
staying and he cooked breakfast. We did not want to discuss the lost traps, we pretended to ourselves and to each
other that we would find them when we went out at the
next low tide. But we knew they were lost, swept up or
downstream by the powerful tides, and I knew I could
never make another eel trap in my life. I knew also that
my partner was taking Adrian with him on a short holiday,
they were leaving that afternoon. They were going to
visit military airfields, and hoped to end up at the Im-
perial War Museum. We ate eggs, bacon and mushrooms
and drank coffee. Sissel's father told me of an idea he had,
a simple but lucrative idea. Shrimps cost very little on the
quayside here and they were very expensive in Brussels.
We could drive two vanloads across there each week, he
was optimistic in his relaxed, friendly way and for a moment I was sure his scheme would work. I drank the last
of my coffee. Well, I said, I suppose that needs some thinking about. I picked up the bucket with the eel in, Sissel and
I could eat that one. My partner told me as we shook
hands that the surest way of killing an eel was to cover it
with salt. I wished him a good holiday and we parted,
still maintaining the silent pretence that one of us would
be rowing out at the next low tide to search for the traps.

After a week at the factory I did not expect Sissel to be
awake when I got home, but she was sitting up in bed,
pale and clasping her knees. She was staring into one
corner of the room. It's in here, she said. It's behind those
books on the floor. I sat down on the bed and took off my
wet shoes and socks. The mouse? You mean you heard

the mouse? Sissel spoke quietly. It's a rat. I saw it run across the room, and it's a rat. I went over to the books and kicked them, and instantly it was out, I heard its claws on the floorboards and then I saw it run along the wall, the size of a small dog it seemed to me then, a rat, a squat, powerful grey rat dragging its belly along the floor. It ran the whole length of the wall and crept behind a chest of drawers. We've got to get it out of here, Sissel wailed, in a voice which was strange to me. I nodded, but I could not move for the moment, or speak, it was so big, the rat, and it had been with us all summer, scrabbling at the wall in the deep, clear silences after our fucking, and in our sleep, it was our familiar. I was terrified, more afraid than Sissel, I was certain the rat knew us as well as we knew it, it was aware of us in the room now just as we were aware of it behind the chest of drawers. Sissel was about to speak again when we heard a noise outside on the stairs, a familiar stamping, machine-gunning noise. I was relieved to hear it. Adrian came in the way he usually did, he kicked the door and leaped in, crouching low, a machine-gun ready at his hip. He sprayed us with raw noises from the back of his throat, we crossed our lips with our fingers and tried to hush him. You're dead, both of you, he said, and got ready for a cartwheel across the room. Sissel shushed him again, she tried to wave him towards the bed. Why sshh? What's wrong with you? We pointed to the chest of drawers. It's a rat, we told him. He was down on his knees at once, peering. A rat? he gasped. Fantastic, it's a big one, look at it. Fantastic. What are you going to do? Let's catch it. I crossed the room quickly and picked up a poker from the fireplace, I could lose my fear in Adrian's excitement, pretend it was just a fat rat in our room, an adventure to catch it. From the bed Sissel wailed again. What are you going to do with that? For a

moment I felt my grip loosen on the poker, it was not just
a rat, it was not an adventure, we both knew that. Meanwhile Adrian danced his dance, Yes, that, use that.
Adrian helped me carry the books across the room, we
built a wall right round the chest of drawers with only one
gap in the middle where the rat could get through. Sissel
went on asking, What are you doing? What are you going
to do with that? but she did not dare leave the bed. We
had finished the wall and I was giving Adrian a coat-
hanger to drive the rat out with when Sissel jumped across
the room and tried to snatch the poker from my hand.
Give me that, she cried, and hung on to my lifted arm. At
that moment the rat ran out through the gap in the books,
it ran straight at us and I thought I saw its teeth bared and
ready. We scattered, Adrian jumped on the table, Sissel
and I were back on the bed. Now we all had time to see the
rat as it paused in the centre of the room and then ran
forward again, we had time to see how powerful and fat
and fast it was, how its whole body quivered, how its tail
slid behind it like an attendant parasite. It knows us, I
thought, it wants us. I could not bring myself to look at
Sissel. As I stood up on the bed, raised the poker and aimed
it, she screamed. I threw it as hard as I could, it struck the
floor point first several inches from the rat's narrow head.
It turned instantly and ran back between the gap in the
books. We heard the scratch of its claws on the floor as it
settled itself behind the chest of drawers to wait.

I unwound the wire coat-hanger, straightened it and
doubled it over and gave it to Adrian. He was quieter now,
slightly more fearful. His sister sat on the bed with her
knees drawn up again. I stood several feet from the gap
in the books with the poker held tight in both hands. I
glanced down and saw my pale bare feet and saw a ghost
rat's teeth bared and tearing nail from flesh. I called out,

Wait, I want to get my shoes. But it was too late, Adrian was jabbing the wire behind the chest of drawers and now I dared not move. I crouched a little lower over the poker, like a batsman. Adrian climbed on to the chest and thrust the wire right down into the corner. He was in the middle of shouting something to me, I did not hear what it was. The frenzied rat was running through the gap, it was running at my feet to take its revenge. Like the ghost rat its teeth were bared. With both hands I swung the poker down, caught it clean and whole smack under its belly, and it lifted clear off the ground, sailed across the room, borne up by Sissel's long scream through her hand in her mouth, it dashed against the wall and I thought in an instant, It must have broken its back. It dropped to the ground, legs in the air, split from end to end like a ripe fruit. Sissel did not take her hand from her mouth, Adrian did not move from the chest, I did not shift my weight from where I had struck, and no one breathed out. A faint smell crept across the room, musty and intimate, like the smell of Sissel's monthly blood. Then Adrian farted and giggled from his held-back fear, his human smell mingled with the wide-open rat smell. I stood over the rat and prodded it gently with the poker. It rolled on its side, and from the mighty gash which ran its belly's length there obtruded and slid partially free from the lower abdomen a translucent purple bag, and inside five pale crouching shapes, their knees drawn up around their chins. As the bag touched the floor I saw a movement, the leg of one unborn rat quivered as if in hope, but the mother was hopelessly dead and there was no more for it.

Sissel knelt by the rat, Adrian and I stood behind her like guards, it was as if she had some special right, kneeling there with her long red skirt spilling round her. She parted the gash in the mother rat with her forefinger and thumb, pushed the bag back inside and closed the blood-spiked fur over it. She remained kneeling a little while and we still stood behind her. Then she cleared some dishes from the sink to wash her hands. We all wanted to get outside now, so Sissel wrapped the rat in newspaper and we carried it downstairs. Sissel lifted the lid of the dustbin and I placed it carefully inside. Then I remembered something, I told the other two to wait for me and I ran back up the stairs. It was the eel I came back for, it lay quite still in its few inches of water and for a moment I thought that it too was dead till I saw it stir when I picked up the bucket. The wind had dropped now and the cloud was breaking up, we walked to the quay in alternate light and shade. The tide was coming in fast. We walked down the stone steps to the water's edge and there I tipped the eel back in the river and we watched him flick out of sight, a flash of white underside in the brown water. Adrian said goodbye to us, and I thought he was going to hug his sister. He hesitated and then ran off, calling out something over his shoulder. We shouted after him to have a good holiday. On the way back Sissel and I stopped to look at the factories on the other side of the river. She told me she was going to give up her job there.

We lifted the mattress on to the table and lay down in front of the open window, face to face, the way we did at the beginning of summer. We had a light breeze blowing in, a distant smoky smell of autumn, and I felt calm, very clear. Sissel said, This afternoon let's clean the room up and then go for a long walk, a walk along the river dyke. I pressed the flat of my palm against her warm belly and said, Yes.

Disguises

Mina that Mina. Soft and breathy now and thick glasses too remembers her last appearance on stage. Sour Goneril at the Old Vic, she took no nonsense, though friends said even then the mind of that Mina was slipping. Prompted, they say, in act one, shouting at the guilty A.S.M. in the interval, and scratched him with her long vermilion nail, below the eye and to the right, a little nick across the cheek. King Lear stepped between, knighted the week before, a household venerate among non-theatregoers, and the director stepped between, flapping at Mina with his programme sheet. 'You royal arse-licker' to one, and 'You backstage pimp' to the other, she spat at each and played one more night. And that to give her understudy time. The last night on stage for Mina, what a grande dame she was sweeping here and there, in and out of cue, a train in a tunnel of blank verse, and her proud unpadded bosom lifting with her caterwaul, and brave. She, near the beginning, carelessly tossed a plastic rose into the front row, and when Lear gave forth she had a fancy business with her fan, it raised a titter from time to time. The audience, sophisticated sentients, felt for her and the melodrama of desperation because they knew about Mina and gave a special cheer at curtain call which sent her weeping to her dressing-room and as she went she pressed the back of her hand into her forehead.

Two days later Brianie died, her sister, Henry's mother, so Mina confusing dates persuaded Mina at the funeral tea, and this is what she told her friends, she gave up the stage to tend her sister's child then ten years old and in need, so Mina told her friends, of a real mother, a Real Mother. And Mina was a surreal mother.

In the drawing-room of her Islington house she drew her nephew to her, pressed his blotchy face into the padded now and scented bosom, and the same again that next day in the taxi to Oxford Street where she bought him a bottle of cologne and a Fauntleroy suit with lace trimmings. In the months she let his hair grow down below the collar and the ears, daring for the early 'sixties, and encouraged him to dress for dinner, the motif of this story, showed him how to mix her drink from the cocktail cabinet in the evening, had a violin teacher round, a dancing-master too, on his birthday a shirt-maker, and then a photographer with a voice pitched politely high. He came to take faded and brown-tinted shots of Henry and Mina posing in costume before the mantelpiece and it was all, Mina told Henry, it was all good training.

Good training for what? Henry did not put this question to her or to himself, not an introspect or sensitive, the kind to accept a new life and this narcissism with no opinion either way, all being part of one fact. The fact was his mother had died, her image six months on was elusive like a faint star. There were details, though, and he questioned them. When the photographer flouncing back and across the room packed his tripod and left, Henry asked Mina, returning from the front door, 'Why does that man have a funny voice?' He was satisfied understanding nothing from Mina. 'I think, darling, because he's queer.' The pictures came soon in heavy packets with Mina running through the kitchen and out for her glasses and shrieking and giggling and tearing at the stiff brown paper with her fingers. They were in gilded oval frames, she passed them across the table to Henry. At the edge the brown faded to nothing, like smoke, precious and unreal, Henry there, wan, impassive, and a straight back, and one hand was resting lightly on Mina's shoulder. She was on the piano stool, skirts spilling around, head lifted back a little, attempting a lady's pout and her hair in a black bun down the nape of her neck. Mina was laughing, excited and getting her other glasses to look at the pictures arm's length, and turning knocked the milk jug over, laughed more and leaping back in her chair to escape the white streams which dribbled to the floor between her legs. And between the laughs, 'What do you think, dear? Aren't they super?' 'They're all right,' said Henry, 'I suppose.'

Good training? Mina did not ask herself either what she meant, but it was to do with the stage if she had, everything Mina did was to do with that. Always on stage even when alone an audience watched and her actions were for them, a kind of superego, she dared not displease them or herself, so sinking with a moan to her bed after some exhaustion, that moan had shape and told. And in the morning sitting to make up her face by the bedroom mirror with a small horseshoe of naked light bulbs around, she felt at her back a thousand eyes and was poised and carried each motion through to its end with a mind to its uniqueness. Henry was not the kind to see the unseen, he mistook Mina. Mina singing, or flinging out her arms, pirouetting in the room, buying parasols and costumes, imitating to the milkman the milkman's accent, or just Mina carrying in a dish from the kitchen to the dining-room table, held out high in front of her and she whistling some military march between her teeth and beating time with strange ballet slippers she always wore, it seemed to

Henry to be for him. He was uneasy, a little unhappy – should he clap, was there something he had to do, join in or Mina might think he was sulking? There were times, catching Mina's mood, he did join in, falteringly, in some celebratory manic around the room. Something then in Mina's eye warned against, said room for one performer only, so he let his steps peter to the nearest chair.

Sure she worried him, but for the rest she was not unkind, tea was ready in the afternoon when he came in from school, special treats, some favourite, custard cakes or toasted buns, and then the talk. Mina sketched out her day's impressions and confidences, more wife in these than aunt, talking fast through mouthfuls blowing out crumbs, and made a crescent moon of grease above the upper lip.

'I saw Julie Frank at lunch Three Tuns she was putting them away still living with that jockey or horse-trainer or whatever and not thinking of marriage but she's a spiteful bitch Henry. "Julie," I said, "now what of these stories you're putting out about Maxine's abortion?" – I told you about that, didn't I! – "Abortion?" she said, "Oh, *that*. All fun and giggles, Mina, nothing more." "Fun and giggles?" I said. "I felt a complete fool when I went round there." "Oooo, did you now?" she said.'

Henry ate the eclairs, nodding quietly and liking to sit down after all day at school to listen to a story, Mina told them so well. Then on the second cup of tea it was Henry's turn to tell his day, more linear and slowly, like this. 'First we had history and then singing and then Mr Carter took us on a walk up Hampstead Hill because he said we were all falling asleep and then it was break and after that we had French and then we had composition.' But it took longer with Mina breaking in with, 'History was *my* favourite subject, I remember ...' and, 'Hampstead Hill is the highest point in London, you must be careful not to fall

off, darling,' and the composition, the story, did he have it
with him? was he going to read it? wait, she must get
comfortable first, now go ahead. Making apologies in his
mind and very reluctant, Henry brought the exercise book
from his satchel, flattened out the pages, began to read, the
monotone of a self-conscious robot, 'No one in the village
ever went near the castle on Grey Crag because of the
terrible cries they heard at midnight ...' At the end Mina
banged the floor with her feet, and clapped, shouted like
someone at the back of a hall, lifted high her teacup, 'We
must get you an agent, dear.' Now it was her turn, she
took the story, reading it back with the right pauses and
piping howls and rattling spoons for effects, convinced him
it was good, even eerie.

This tea and confession could be two hours; when it
was over they went to their rooms, it was dressing for
dinner. Later than September Henry found his fire lit a
waving glow and writhing furniture shadows on the
wall, his suit or costume unfolded on the bed, whichever
Mina chose that night for him to wear. Dressing for dinner.
It allowed two hours or so for Mrs Simpson to let herself
in with her own key, cook the meal and let herself out,
Mina to bathe and with black goggles lie beneath her
artificial sun, Henry to do his homework, read his old
books, play with his old junk. Mina and Henry together
found old books and charts in damp bookshops near the
British Museum, collected junk from the Portobello
Road and Camden market, the we buy and sell everything
shops of Kentish Town. A queue of yellow-eyed elephants
diminishing, carved in wood, a still working clockwork
train of painted tin, puppets with no strings, a scorpion
pickled in a jar. And a Victorian children's theatre giving
instructions from a polite booklet for two people to play
scenes from the *Thousand and One Nights*. For two months

they pushed the faded cardboard figures across the
variable backdrops, you change them with a flick of your
wrist, banging knives on teaspoons for sword fights, and
Mina got tense crouching on her knees there, angry sometimes when he missed the cue – he often did – but she
missed them too, and then they laughed. Mina could do
the voices, the villain's master's prince's heroine's plain-
tiff's voices, and tried to teach him how, but uselessly and
they laughed again for Henry could do two, a high one
and a low one. Mina tired of the cardboard theatre, now
only Henry took it out before the fire and, shy, let the
figures speak in his mind. Twenty minutes before the dinner he took off his school clothes, washed, took up the
costume Mina had planned and joined her in the dining-
room where she waited in her costume.

Mina collected them, costumes, guises, outfits, old
clothes, wherever she could get them and she sewed them
into shape, packing three wardrobes. And now for Henry
too. A few suits from Oxford Street, but the rest unwanted
stock, from amateur theatre groups which were folding
up, forgotten pantomimes, seconds from the best costu-
miers, it was her hobby, you see. To dinner Henry wore a
soldier's uniform, and a lift-boy's from an American hotel
before the war, he must be an old man now, a kind of
monk's habit and a shepherd's smock from the Virgilian
Eclogues, performed once and eurhythmically by the girls
of the upper sixth, written by or arranged by the head
prefect, who Mina was once. Henry was uncurious, obe-
dient, put on each evening what he found at the foot of his
bed, and found Mina downstairs in bustle or whalebone
hoops, sequined cat suit, or become a Crimean war nurse.
But she was not different nor did she play a part to her
costume, she made no comment on either's appearance,
seemed in fact to want to forget the matter, eat the meal,

relax, drink from the glass her nephew passed her, so he was trained. Henry took the routine, enjoyed the ritual of the long tea and structured privacy, beginning to wonder on the way home from school what was ready for him to wear, hope to find something new on his bed. But Mina was mysterious, not warning over tea of something new, let him discover it and smiled to herself while he mixed her drink and poured himself a lemonade, standing there in a toga she found, toasting with their glasses across the large room, silently. She turned him round, making to herself some note of an alteration, then started the meal, the usual chatter and stories of her days on the stage, or other people's stories. All so very strange, somehow to Henry ordinary, homely in winter.

One afternoon retiring after tea, opening the door of his room Henry found a girl lying face down across his bed; stepping a little closer, it was not a girl it was a kind of party frock and a wig of long blonde hair, white tights, black leather slippers. Catching his breath he touched the dress, cold, ominously silky, it rustled when he picked it up, all flounces and frills, layer on layer with white satin and lace edged with pink, a cute bow falling at the back. He let it fall back on the bed, the most girlish thing he ever saw, wiped his hand on his trousers, not daring to touch the wig which seemed alive. Not these, not him, did Mina really want him to? He stared miserably at the bed and picked up the white tights, not these, surely. All right being a soldier, a Roman, a pageboy, something like that, but not a girl, it was wrong to be a girl. Like the best of Henry's friends at school he did not care for girls, avoided their huddles and intrigues, their whispers and giggles and holding hands and passing notes and I love I love, they set his teeth on edge to see. Unhappily Henry paced the room, sat at his desk to work at memorizing French words,

armoire cupboard *armoire* cupboard *armoire* cupboard
armoire ...? and glanced across his shoulder every minute
to see if they were still there on the bed, and they were.
Twenty minutes to dinner, it could not be right, he could
not take his own clothes off or put those on, and yet a terrible thing to upset the ritual of the dressing-up, and now
he could hear Mina singing as she left the bathroom, she was
doing up her face in the next room. Could he ask to wear
something else, when she had been out today to buy him
this, when yesterday she told him how good wigs cost and
were hard to come by? Sitting on that end of the bed
farthest from the clothes and wanting to cry, for the first
time in months he missed his mother, solid and always the
same, typing at the Ministry of Transport. He heard Mina
pass the door going downstairs to wait for him and he
began to loosen his shoe and then not, he did not want to.
Mina called up to him nothing different in her voice,
'Henry, darling, are you coming down?' and he said out
loud, 'Just a moment.' But he could not move, could not
touch those things, did not want to, even if only for pretend, appear a girl. Now there were her footsteps on the
stairs, she was coming to see, he pulled one shoe off in
token palliation, there was nothing he could do.

She came into his room dressed, he had not seen her
wear it before, an officer's uniform, brisk, straight-lined,
thin buckle epaulettes, and a red stripe in the trousers, her
hair pinned back, perhaps it was greased, shiny black
shoes, and her face with a man's heavy lines, the hint of a
moustache. She marched across the room, 'But darling,
you haven't started to get ready yet, let me help you, it will
need tying at the back anyway,' and she began to loosen
his tie. Henry stood too numb to resist, she was so certain,
pulling off his shirt, trousers, the other shoe, his socks, and
then strangely his underpants. Had he washed yet? She

took him by the wrist, steered him to the washbasin, was
filling it with warm water and flanneling his face, drying it,
sweeping him along in a frenzy of her own, a special
momentum. He stood naked in the centre of the room in a
horror dream while Mina rummaged on the bed among
the clothes and found them, turning from the bed with
them in her hand, a pair of white knickers, and Henry
said 'No' to himself as they came towards. Bending down
by his feet, 'Lift one leg,' she said cheerily and knocked on
one foot with the back of her hand, to which he could not
stir, just stood, frightened by the edge of impatience in her
voice, 'Come on, Henry, or dinner will be spoiled.' He
moved his tongue before he spoke, 'No, I don't want to
wear those.' For a moment her back held there bent over
by his feet, then she straightened, caught his forearm in a
pinching mean grip and was looking close in his face,
sucking him in with her look. He saw the mask of makeup
wadded on, an old man, the lines of frivolous scars and her
lower lip stretched with anger across her teeth, first in his
legs and then everywhere he began to tremble. She shook
his arm, hissed, 'Lift one leg', and waited while he made
the beginnings of the movement, but that movement
released him, let fall a trickle of urine down his leg. She
pushed him to the sink again, wiping him quickly with the
towel and said, 'Now', so that too frightened, too humilia-
ted, to refuse Henry lifted one leg and then the other, submitted to the cold layers of the dress against his skin,
lowered over his head, laced from behind, then the tights,
the leather slippers, and last the close-fitting wig, the gold
hair fell past both his eyes, tumbled freely across his
shoulders.

In the mirror he saw her, a sickeningly pretty little
girl, he glanced away and followed miserably Mina downstairs, rustling sulkily and still shaking in his legs. Mina

was gay now, she made conciliatory jokes about his reluctance this evening, spoke of a trip somewhere, Battersea funfair perhaps, and even Henry in his confusion knew she was excited by his presence and appearance, for twice in the meal she got up from her place to come to kiss and hug him where he sat and run her fingers through the fabric, 'All is forgiven, all is forgiven.' Later Mina drank three glasses of port and sprawled herself in the armchair, a drunken soldier calling to his girl, wanted her to come and sit on this officer's knee. Henry stayed out of reach, small panics in his stomach at each thought that Mina – was she very wicked or very mad? he could not decide, but for sure the dressing-up game loses its fun by this, he sensed some compulsion in it for Mina, he dared not contradict it, there was something dark – the way she pushed him, the way she hissed, something he did not understand and he pushed it from his mind. So towards the end of the evening, escaping Mina's hands to pull him on her knee, and catching glimpses of himself in the many mirrors in that room, reflections of the pretty little blonde girl in her party frock, he told himself, 'It's for her, it's nothing to do with anything, it's for her, it's nothing to do with me.'

Afraid of the thing in her he did not understand. Henry for the most part liked her, she was his friend, she wanted to make him laugh, not to tell him what to do. She made him laugh with all her funny voices, and if she told a story and was excited, and that was often, she acted it out for him, telling it up and down the length of the sitting-room. 'The day Deborah left her husband she walked straight down to the bus stop ...' and here Mina danced a little arm-swinging march into the centre of the room ... 'but it was only *then* that she remembered that at lunchtime there were no buses from the village ...' shading her eyes with her hand she scoured the room for a bus, then the other hand flew to her mouth, wide eyes, jaw sagging, remembrance came all over her face, like the sun from behind a cloud … 'so she went back home to have her lunch …' again the little walk … 'and there was her husband sitting in front of two empty plates, belching away and saying, "Well, I didn't expect you home so I ate yours" ' … hands on her hips Mina bulged her eyes at Henry who was now the husband sitting at the table, and he wondering if he should join in, lean back in his chair and belch. But he laughed instead because Mina was laughing now, she always did when she came to the end of her story. Mina was on television now and then, he admired her for that, even though it was only the commercials, she was usually the housewife with the right soap powder, curlers, and knotted scarf in her hair gabbling over a garden wall, some neighbour leaned over and asked about her sheets, what was her secret, and Mina told her in her Souf Lunnun accent. She hired the set just for the ads, they sat there with the schedule sheet waiting for it to come on and when it did they laughed. When it was over she turned it off, only sometimes did they watch a programme, and then it was the actors, they made her angry in advance, 'Christ! that's Paul Cook, I knew him when he swept the floor at the Ipswich rep,' she jumped up from her chair, unplugged the set on the way to the kitchen, Henry sat in his chair watching the white dot recede in the centre of the screen.

One afternoon nearing a Christmas, coming cold and late from school, there was a pile near his plate at tea, arranged by Mina and he was bound to find them, of smooth white cards, reading in elaborate copperplate, lean and decorous, Mina and Henry invite you to their party. Come disguised. RSVP. Henry read several, his own unfamiliar name in print, and looked across at Mina watching him, some kind of pursed-up smile hovering in the space between them, all ready to break out and she was waiting for him. Excited but unable to show it because he was waited for, so lamely he said, 'That's very nice,' and that was wrong, that was not how he felt it at all, never been to a party and never been on an invitation card. Still something in Mina made it hard to say, more was required, 'Disguises though, what kind of disguises?' But too late because Mina was laughing and rising while he said it, and making a strutting ballerina walk across the room and chanting in time to her steps, '*That's* nice? Ni-ice? Ni-ice? Ni-ice?' and so round the room back to the table and the chair where he sat watching her and very unsure. She stood behind his chair tousling his hair for pretend affection, but pulling it, and stung his eyes. 'Henry, dear, it will be formidable, fantastical, awful, but never nice, nothing we ever do will be nice,' speaking this all the while she ran her hands in his hair, twined it through her fingers. He turned to look upwards and escape her, and she was caught in the sudden wild upward stare in the large white of his eyes, relented now, squeezed him with real affection, 'We'll have the time of our lives, aren't you excited? What do you think of the cards?' He took the cards again, saying seriously, 'No one will dare not come.' The edge of the vicious gone from her tone she told him, pouring the tea, that the disguises must be impenetrable, and made jokes and anecdotes about the friends she was going to invite.

After dinner they sat by the coal fire talking, Mina wearing a New Look of the rationing days and Henry in his Fauntleroy suit, Mina said suddenly after a long silence, 'And you? Who are you going to invite?' He did not reply for several minutes, thinking of his friends at

school. At school he was different, it was different, he
played chasing games and loud football against the wall,
and in class borrowed some of Mina's words and anecdotes
to make his own; the teachers considered him mildly
precocious. He had many friends, but he wandered and
did not have a best friend like some of them. And then at
home sitting quietly through the drama spectacles and
Mina's moods, attending so not to miss a cue, he had not
thought of the two things together, one large and free with
big windows, lino floors, long rows of pegs to hang your
coat on, the other was dense, the things in his room, two
cups of tea and Mina's games. Telling his day to Mina was
like telling a dream over breakfast, true and not true, at
last he said, 'I don't know, I can't think of anyone.' Could
the ones he played football with be in the same room as
Mina? 'Have you not made any friends at school worth
bringing home?' Henry did not make an answer. How
could they be in disguises, costumes and things like that,
he was sure it would not fit.

She did not ask him again the next day, but unwound
the details, ideas which flooded to her, all day thinking of
nothing else. To help the disguises along the rooms shall
be dimly lit. 'Even best friends won't be able to recognize
each other,' and disguises must stay a secret, no one will
know who Mina is, she can move around, have a good
time, let them get their own drinks, do their own intro-
ducing – false names of course – and they are all theatre
people, masters of disguise, masters at the art of creating
character, because that is the art of acting as Mina sees it,
creating a self, in other words a disguise. And breathlessly
on and on with the details, it came to her in the bath, of
course red light bulbs, a special recipe for punch, arrange
the music from somewhere and perhaps we will burn some
joss sticks. Then the invitations were sent away, all the

arrangements made that could be made and it was still
two weeks, so Mina and therefore Henry spoke of the
thing no more. Since she knew his costumes, had bought
them all herself and did not want to know him on the day,
she gave him money for his disguise, he must get it himself
and promise to hold it to himself. Walking all one Saturday he found it in a junk shop near the Highbury and
Islington tube station, among the cameras, broken shavers,
and yellow books, a kind of monstrous Boris Karloff face
of cloth with holes for the eyes and mouth, and in the
shape of a hood you pulled it over your head. It had wiry
hair in all directions, it was funny and surprised, not
frightening, though, cost thirty shillings, the man said.
And not having his money with him that day he told the
man he would be along to collect it Monday when he
came from school.

But that day he was not there, that day he met Linda, it
was the way the desks were arranged, in pairs, four by
four and a gangway to walk down. Henry was the newest
to the class, proud to have a desk to himself, that was the
way it worked out when all the others had to share. His
charts and books and two puppets took both sides of it,
good to sit at the back all spread out. The teacher explaining twenty-five feet said that it was about from here to
Henry's desk, and they turned round to look at everyone
in the class, of course it was his desk. On Monday there
was a girl, a new girl, and sitting at his desk, setting out
her coloured pencils as if she belonged. Seeing him stare
she turned her look down, said quietly but with no sub-
mission, 'Teacher told me to sit here,' and Henry scowled,
sat down, his space violated was bad, and this was a girl.
Through the first three lessons she sat, a no presence, by
his side, and Henry stared ahead, for looking round was to

admit her, these seeking girls who meet your eye. At break he rose before the others, stood under the stairs drinking milk, avoiding his friends, and waited till the classroom was empty to go back in there to clear one half of his table for her, sulkily, packing the bits, the tender off the clockwork train, some old clothes and things, into two carrier bags, and feeling obscurely martyred put them behind her chair, he wanted her to know how the inconvenience was. She made a nervous little smile coming in to sit down but he was brisk, a pretender, dismissive, looking away and rubbing his hands.

But bad temper fades and he became curious, stole some glances and then again some more, the striking things about her moved something, like the long fine sun-yellow hair all over her shoulders on the soft wool about her back, and bloodless skin like this paper but almost transparent, and then her nose, very stretched, tight and taut, flared like a horse, her scared large grey eyes. Knowing him watching her again she made the beginnings of a smile with the corner of her lips, gave Henry a little uneasy thrill, that movement, in the pit of his stomach, so he moved his eyes to the front of the classroom, understanding vaguely what it was when they said this or that girl was beautiful, when it always seemed before an exaggeration Mina might make.

Growing up you fell in love, Henry knew that, with some girl you met, and that was when you got married, but only if you met a girl you liked, and how for him when most girls could not be understood? This one, though, he could see her elbow almost on to his part of the desk, this one was frail and different, he wanted to touch her neck or put his foot near hers, or did Henry feel guilty with all this new, this confusion and feeling? A history lesson and all drawing a map of Norway and colouring Viking ships with their bows pointing south. He touched her elbow, 'Can I borrow a blue pencil?' 'Blue for the sea or blue for the sky?' 'Blue for the sea.' She found a pencil for him, told him her name was Linda, and holding it still warm from her own hand he bent over his own map with extra care, scratched a blue halo for his coastline making it sound *linda linda* as he worked it up and down three inches from his eyes. Then he remembered, 'I'm Henry' he whispered, the grey eyes opened wider to take it in, 'Henry?' 'Yes.' Frightened by himself he steered round her at lunch, made sure of another table to eat his meal and noisily sought out his friends across the playground who taunted, 'See you got a girl,' for which he pantomimed a tremor of real disgust to make them laugh and take him in. They played football against the playground wall and Henry shouted most, swung his elbows and fists, but when the ball went over the wall and they hung about waiting, then his mind was gone on in advance into the classroom sitting next to a girl. And returning himself he found her already there and let her see by the slightest incline of his head he saw her smile. The afternoon trickled out bored and slow, he shifted around in his seat not wanting it to end or continue, knowing she was sitting there.

He knelt behind her chair when school was over, making as if to look for something in the bags, certain he would not see her till the morning. She was still sitting at the desk, completing something and not noticing, so Henry rustled the bags some more, standing up cleared his throat, said roughly, 'See you, then,' echoing his voice in the empty classroom. She stood up, closing her book, 'I can carry one.' Taking one of the bags from him she led the way out of the room and they crossed the silent playground, Henry looking round to see if his friends were still about. There was a woman by the school gates with a leather coat and her hair was tied in a ponytail, young and old at the same time, who bent down to Linda and kissed her on the lips. She said, 'Have you made a friend already?' looking at Henry, he stood a few paces off. Linda said simply, 'His name is Henry,' and called to him, 'She's my mother,' and her mother stretched out her hand towards Henry who came over and shook it, very grown-up. 'Hello, Henry, can we give you a ride home with your bags?' described with a vague tossing of her wrist joint the big black car parked behind her. She put his bags in the back seat, suggested they all sit in the front, which they did, and Linda pressed close up against him to let her mother change the gears. He was not expected home straight away because of the mask, he had told Mina he would be late, he accepted then the invitation to tea and sat pressed along the car door, listened to Linda tell her mother of her first day at the new school. Down a gravel curving driveway they stopped by a large house of red brick and trees all round and through the trees the Heath dropping down in one long sweep towards a lake, which Linda pointed to when they walked round the side of the house. 'The mansion there, you can just make it out in the trees, that's Kenwood House, it's got lots of old pictures you can see for free. They have Rembrandt's "Self-Portrait" in there, the most famous picture in the world.' Henry wondered what about the Mona Lisa, but he was very impressed.

Her mother made the tea, Linda took Henry to show him her room, along a corridor with thick carpets which muffled their steps, it opened into the hallway at the foot of a wide stairway, split half way up in two directions on to the great landing, a horseshoe expanse with a grandfather clock at one end, at the other a massive chest covered in brass with figures stamped upon it. It was a trousseau chest, Linda told him, where they put gifts for the bride, it was four hundred years old. They went up another staircase, did all the house belong to them? 'It used to be Daddy's but he went away so now it's Mummy's.' 'Where did he go?' 'He wanted to marry someone else instead of Mummy so they had a divorce.' 'And so he gave your m-mother this house to make up for it.' He could not bring himself to say 'mummy'. It was a junk heap with a bed, Linda's room, covered the floor and blocked the doorway, toy prams, dolls, their clothes, games and bits of games, a big blackboard on the wall and the bed unmade, the sheets trailing into the centre of the room, beyond that the pillow, bottles and brushes in front of a dressing mirror and all the walls pink, alien girlish, it excited him. 'Don't you have to tidy it up?' 'This morning we had a pillow fight. I like it untidy, don't you.' Henry followed Linda down the stairs, it is always much better to do just what you want if you can find a place to do it.

She said at tea, Linda's mother, to call her Claire, and later asking him if there was something else and he said, 'No thank you, Claire,' it made Linda choke on a mouthful of drink and Henry and Claire pounded her back, they went on after that laughing at nothing at all, Linda clutched at Henry to keep herself from falling on the floor. A tall man, in the middle of all this, put his head round the kitchen door, he had thick black eyebrows, he smiled, 'Enjoying yourselves,' and disappeared. When Henry put on his coat to leave and asked Linda who that man was, she told him it was Theo who sometimes came to stay with them, and whispered, 'He sleeps in Mummy's bed.' As he spoke them, wishing the words back, he asked, 'What for?' and made Linda giggle into the wall of coats. They all three sat in the front again, squashed up close, and after a little way Linda wanted them to sing 'Frère Jacques' which they did all the distance to Islington so loud the people in

their cars could hear them when they stopped at the
traffic lights, smiling at them through their car windows.
The singing broke off when Claire pulled up at Henry's
house, it was suddenly very quiet. He reached over to the
back seat for his bags, muttering thanks for having ...
but Claire interrupted would he like to come on Sunday,
and Linda shouted that it must be for the whole day, till
they were all talking at once, Claire, if he wanted she
could pick him up in the car, Linda, promised to take him
to see the pictures in Kenwood House, Henry, that he
must ask Mina first but he was sure it was all right. Linda
squeezed his hand, 'See you at school,' shouting, waving,
the beginnings of another chorus lost in the roar of a
passing lorry, they left him there on the pavement with his
bags, waiting a while before he went inside.

Mina was sitting at the table, her head was in her hands,
the tea things were all around her. She did not look round
at his hello, he lingered uneasily in the doorway, taking off
his coat, fussing with the bags. Mina said quietly, 'Where
have you been?' He looked at the clock, it was ten to six,
he was an hour and thirty-five minutes late. 'I told you I
was going to be an hour late.' 'An hour?' she drawled
slowly, 'it's almost two hours now.' There was something
familiar in Mina's strangeness, he felt his legs begin to go
weak. At the table he began to play with a teaspoon,
squeezing it into a tunnel made by his knuckles, till Mina
drew air sharply through her nostrils. 'Put that down,' she
snapped, 'I asked you where have you been?' Trembling
in his voice, he explained, the mother of a school friend
invited him home for tea and – 'I thought you were picking
up your costume,' she spoke very softly. 'Well, I was
but ...' Henry stared down at his fingers spread out on the
table. 'And if you were going to someone's house why

couldn't you let me know?' Now she yelled at the top of her voice, 'We got a bloody telephone.' Neither spoke, Mina's echo lasted five minutes in the room, still chiming in his head, and then she said quietly, 'You don't give a damn anyway. Go up and get changed.' There were things he knew he could say and make it all right, but none of the words was in his head, all that was were the things he could see, his knuckles, the pattern of the cloth beneath them filled his attention, nothing to say. Walking behind Mina's chair to the door, she turned to hold him by the elbow, 'And this time no fuss,' and then pushed him away. At the top of the stairs he thought of what she had said, no fuss, some new costume for humiliation, for being late and breaking with the afternoon ritual. He approached the girl laid neatly on the bed, the same girl as before. Without thought he took his clothes off, could not bring to the open again Mina's frenzy, the vicious compulsion to make a stranger of her, then he was frightened of her, feared it now and shivered, pulling the cold material over his skin, and the white tights, hurrying in case she thought he was hesitating. He fumbled with the thin leather laces, his fingers were pursued, and took up the wig, standing in front of the mirror to adjust it, standing there he glanced up, his motions froze, again that movement in his belly's pit, for there she was in his bedroom now, the hair falling freely about the back, her pale taut skin, her nose. He took the hand mirror from the basin, watched his face from all sides, the eyes were coloured different, his were bluer and his nose a little larger. But it was the first glance, the shock of the first glance was still with him. He removed the wig, it was clownish, his short black hair with the party frock, it made him laugh. He put the wig back on, did a short dance across the room, Henry and Linda at once, closer than in the car, inside her now and she was in him. It was no longer an oppression, he was free of Mina's anger, invisible inside this girl. He began to brush out the wig, the way he saw Linda do it when she came in from school, starting from the end and downwards, so not to split the ends she told him.

He was in front of the mirror still when she came into the room suddenly, the same officer's uniform, her face even harder than last time, she turned him by the shoulders so he faced away from her, then she tied the dress from behind, humming softly beneath her breath. She too combed out the wig, ran her hand up the inside of his leg to feel his underwear, and, satisfied, spun him round to face her so he felt the same immobile fear seeing close to the black heavy lines of her made-up face, the straight rods of greased hair. She leaned over him, pulled him in close, kissing his forehead, 'You'll do,' and led him by the hand downstairs in silence, and this time it was she who poured the drinks, two full glasses of red wine. She bowed, delivered the glass to his hand and clicking her heels and saying in a mock gruff voice, 'There you are, my dear.' He held the unusual glass, its long tinted stem was too short for his whole fist, he held it in both hands. On special occasions Mina mixed him shandy, and the rest was always lemonade. Now Mina stood with her back to the fire, shoulders well back, the glass level with her flattened chest, 'Cheers,' and swallowed two large mouthfuls, 'drink up.' He wet the end of his tongue, held down the shudder of bittersweet, then closing his eyes took in a mouthful, pushing it to the back of his throat quickly with his tongue and this way avoided all the taste but for something furry left behind in his mouth as aftertaste. Mina finished her wine, was waiting now for him to finish his, and took his empty glass to fill at the cabinet, set the wine on the table, and began to fetch the dishes. Dizzy and unreal he helped carry a dish from the hotplate, wondering at Mina's silence. They sat down, Linda and Henry, Henry and Linda. Through the meal Mina lifted her glass saying, 'Cheers,' waiting for him to lift his before drinking, and once she got up to pour more wine. It was sliding from him now, all the things he looked at drifting away from themselves and yet staying at the same time, the space between objects undulated, Mina's face splintered moved and merged with its images, so he gripped the edge of the table to steady the room and saw Mina see him do this, saw her jagged smile meant to be encouragement, saw her drift heavily away to fetch the coffee pot against the movement of the room haled on its three axes, and if he closed his eyes if you close your eyes you might fall off the edge of the world, it tilts upwards beginning somewhere near your feet. And through all this Mina was saying, Mina was wanting to know something, what about his afternoon, what had he done in the other house, so that to tell her he gathered his tongue from whatever it was, heard his own voice come faintly in on him from the next room, the glue on the roof of his mouth, 'We and ... we took out, she took us ...' till he gave up, submitting to Mina's braying and barking and laughing, 'Oh my poor little girl's had a little too much,' and as she was saying this was lurching toward him, lifted him under the armpits half carried him half dragged him to the armchair pulling him there on to her lap and turned his body to make his legs hang over the chair's side, cradled his head in her arms pressed tight hot and all over him like a wrestler, he could not move his arms and legs together to free himself, she had him tight she pressed his face hard between the gap of her unbuttoned tunic, so spinning there in her arms he knew to move suddenly was to be suddenly sick. She seemed to want this girl and pushed his face closer to her breast, for there was nothing beneath the tunic, nothing but Henry's face against the faintly scented corrugated skin of her limp old dugs and her hand was cupped by the back of his neck, he could not move out of the brown tissue, dared not jerk suddenly, he knew what was in his stomach, could not stir even when she began to sing and her other hand began to wander in the layers of his dress in and around his thigh, she half said, she half sang, 'A soldier needs a girl, a soldier needs a girl,' trailing off to the rhythm of her breathing becoming ever sharper ever deeper and Henry rose and fell with it, felt himself pulled closer, opened his eyes into the grey-blue pallor of Mina's breasts, grey and blue the way he imagined a dead person's face. 'Sick,' he murmured into her body and out of his mouth slid noiselessly a brown-red mess of dinner and wine, colour for the death pallor inside the tunic. He rolled off her no longer held, on to the floor with the wig slipping from his head, red and brown stains streaked the fresh white and pink all tawdry now, he pulled the wig completely clear, 'I'm Henry,' said thickly. Mina did not move for a while, sat staring at the wig where it lay on the floor, then getting up she stepped over Henry, upstairs, and from his spinning room he could hear her run the bath water, and just sat where he landed, watched the moving carpet patterns between his fingers, he felt better for being sick, he could not move.

Mina returned from her bath in an everyday dress, herself now, and helped him to his feet, led him by the fire where she untied the dress, taking it in the kitchen to soak in a bucket. She gathered up the wig, took his hand, and taught him how to walk the stairs, singsonging each one as for a child, 'One and two and three and ...' In his bedroom he swayed against her shoulder while she took the rest of his clothes, found his pyjamas while she was talking all the time, the time *she* got drunk for the first ... well the next day she couldn't remember a *thing*, and Henry, not sure of what she was saying but the tone was fine, recognized it like her dress, he lay on his back in bed her hand on his forehead to stay the room a little, while Mina sang and spoke the song from downstairs, 'A soldier needs a girl like a lion needs a mane, To murmur in his ear and kiss away the pain.' She stroked his hair, and when he woke up the following day the wig was beside him on the pillow, it must have fallen off in the night.

Waking up he thought of Linda, and the pain behind his eyes, and how there was some feeling in the room it was no longer morning. Downstairs Mina said, 'Do you want some lunch, I let you sleep it off,' but he was dressed for school, taking his satchel from its hook, out the door and across the street with Mina calling after him to come back, the damp wind was free in his hair, the night before a confusion but, he was certain, Mina had forfeited something by it that made it easy now to run from her fading voice. To Linda. At the school he made his excuses, a sickness and that was not untrue, he was still white enough this afternoon to be believed. To his desk for the beginning of the afternoon classes, where she was waiting smiling as he came towards, ready to press a note in his hand, a scrap reading, 'Are you coming Sunday?' He turned it and wrote yes, in the same spirit he had run free this morning, held it under the table for her to take it with her fingers which came locking into his and did not let go a moment or two, gripped and slid away. In his stomach the pit, in his groin a little blood stirring in a pre-pubertal skin, pushed up like spring flowers, into the folds of his clothes and the note fell unnoticed to the floor.

Could he tell her of glancing in the mirror, Henry and Linda fused by appearances, how they were one at once and he felt free and did a dance before Mina came in, he wanted to tell her, but all the other explaining too, about Mina; where could you begin, how are games which are not really games explained? Instead he told her of the mask he was to buy that afternoon, a kind of monster, 'But more to make you laugh than run away,' and that meant he told her of the party, his name was on the invitation card with Mina's, all disguised and no one knows who you are, anyone can do what they want because it doesn't matter. They were in the playground, empty after everyone had left, they made stories about the things you can do when no one knows who you are. Did she want to come? she did, she wanted to very much. Her mother was crossing the playground towards them, she kissed Linda, put her hand on Henry's shoulder, and they all walked to the car. Linda told her mother of Henry's mask and Henry's party, Claire told her she could go, it sounded fun. They said goodbye.

He was at the shop out of breath, not wanting to be late home again for Mina. The man behind the counter, he had a way with little boys, a jovial unfunny way, 'Where's the fire?' he said when Henry came in his shop, and trying to put over his urgency, Henry told him quickly, 'I've come about the mask.' The shop man leaned slowly across the counter, his joke quivering about the corner of his lips, he could hardly wait to say it. 'S'funny, I thought you had it on,' and watched Henry's face, waiting for his laugh to fall in with his own. Henry smiled for him, 'You said you would keep it for me.' 'Let's see,' making a great show of tracing the figures on the calendar, 'if I'm not mistaken,' he held his breath and drawled out, 'if I'm not mistaaaken today is Tuesday.' He beamed at Henry his customer, arched his eyebrows, watching his customer fidget, 'Have you still got it?' and still with his eyebrows raised he was pointing one finger in the air, a goon amusing no one, 'Now that's the point, have I still got it?' While Henry began to understand how violence was done he was reaching under the counter, 'Let me see, what have we here,' and brought the mask out, Henry's mask. 'Can you wrap it for me, you see it has to be kept a secret.' The man, Henry saw for the first time, was an old man and he felt a little sorry. The man carefully wrapped his mask in two layers of stiff brown paper and found him an old string bag to carry it in. He was silent now, Henry wished he would go on with the bad jokes, at least he could understand those. The only other word he said was 'There,' handing the bag to Henry across the counter. Henry called goodbye as he left the shop but the man had gone into the back room, he did not hear him.

Mina said nothing of the evening before, she cut slices of cake for him instead and talked a lot and fast, made a quick humorous reference to the way he left the house, she was back to herself. In the kitchen Henry saw the dress in a bucket of water, like a rare dead fish. He spoke with hesitation, 'This friend of mine, the family has asked me to spend the day with them on Sunday,' and Mina was distant, 'Really, have I met your friend, why don't you ask him to the party?' 'I already have and they want me to go there on Sunday,' why was it important not to mention the sex of his friend? Mina was vague, 'We'll see,' but he was there behind her, following her out to the kitchen, 'You see I have to let them know tomorrow,' and by the turn of his voice demanded of the silence which followed, an answer. She smiled, she brushed the hair from his eyes with her hand, friendly and resigned she said, 'I think not, darling. Now what about the homework you missed last night,' propelling him gently to the foot of the stairs where he stepped to one side, 'But they asked me to go, I want to go.' Mina was cheery, 'I don't think so really, darling.' 'I want to go.' She took her hand off his shoulder, she sat on the bottom step, chin on her hands, and she was thinking for a long time, and then, 'And what am I meant to do on Sunday when you're off with all your friends?' This sudden change, he was the giver when before he was the asker, he was standing and she was sitting by his feet, there was nothing to say, he was numb. After a while she said, 'Well?' stretching her hands towards him, he moved a little closer till he was where she could take both his hands in hers, and she looked at him over her glasses, she took them off, and he saw then the moisture collecting in her eyes' rims. That was wrong, that was a terrible thing, a terrible weight on him now he felt, can people be so important? She squeezed his hands tighter, 'All right,' he said, 'I'll stay.'

By his arms she tried to bring him closer but he shook his hands free, stepping round her to run upstairs. He took the brown suit from his bed and hung it on the chair, lay on the bed on his back, pushed the image of Linda away, guiltily. Mina came in, she sat by his shoulder staring into his face while he avoided hers, he did not want to see her eyes again, and she just sat playing with the corner of the blanket, pinching it between her finger and thumb. Mina combed his hair with her fingers, he went stiff inside waiting for her to stop, he did not like her fingers near his face, not now. 'Are you angry with me, dear?' He shook his head, still not looking in her face. 'You are angry with me, I can tell.' She stood by the table picking up from it a piece of rough wood, he was carving it now for months, intended as a swordfish, he could not give it power or sinuosity to its trunk, it was still a piece of wood only, a child's representation of Fish. Mina turned and turned it in her hand, looking at it, not seeing it. In the

ceiling, there was the big stairway which split in two ways
half way up and Linda and Claire pillow-fighting in the
bedroom, probably Claire wanted to cheer Linda up
because it was her first day at school, and the tall man with
thick eyebrows, he slept in the same bed as Claire. Mina
said, 'You really want to go, don't you?' Henry said, 'It
doesn't matter, really it's not that important.' Mina turned
the wood in her hand, 'You want to go, so you go.' Henry
sat up, he was not quite old enough to know the special
games that people might like to play, he was not old
enough so he said, 'All right then, I'll go.' Mina left the
room, the powerless swordfish in her hand still.

Henry lifted the heavy knocker and let it fall against the
white door. Claire led him down the dark corridor to the
kitchen, 'Linda spends most of Sunday mornings in bed,'
they emerged in the fluorescent light of the kitchen, 'you
can go up and play with her but first you can talk to me
and have a hot drink.' He let her take his coat, he turned
round for her to admire his new suit, 'We must find you
some clothes to play in.' She made him a chocolate drink,
she carried him along with her talk, he was not on his
guard against sudden surprises. She was pleased he was a
friend of Linda's, she said so, and said how Linda talked
about him all the time, 'She's made a painting of you and a
drawing, but she won't show them to you, I know.' She
wanted to know about him so he told her about the things
he collected from junk shops, the cardboard theatre and
all the old books, and then about Mina, how she was good
at telling stories because she used to be on the stage, he
had never spoken so much in one go before and he was
going to tell her everything, the dressing up and the getting
drunk, but he held back, he was not sure how to say it and
he wanted her to like him, perhaps she wouldn't if he told

her how drunk he was and sick over Mina. She brought
him some play clothes, a light-blue sweater and a faded
pair of jeans which belonged to Linda, did he mind
wearing them, she asked him, and he smiled and said no.
She left the kitchen to answer the phone, calling behind her
that he should find his own way up to Linda's room, back
down the dark corridor leading to the foot of the stairs, he
could not understand why there were no lights except at
either end. On the landing he stopped by the massive
chest, traced with his finger the figures in the brass, a
procession with the rich people up front, perhaps relatives
of the married couple, all filling out the street and the
pavements with their costumes billowing out behind, all
with their backs straight and proud, and then after them
the townspeople, just a rabble, each with a wine cup in his
hand, tottering and grabbing at his neighbour, drunk and
laughing at the ones in front. Near him there was a door
open and he looked in, a bedroom, the biggest he had ever
seen, a large double bed in the middle not against any
wall. Taking a few paces into the room, the bed was unmade, bunched up in the middle, and he could see now
there was a man asleep face downwards, he froze, then
walked backwards quickly out into the landing closing the
door quietly behind. He remembered Linda's clothes left
on the trunk, found them, and ran up the second staircase to Linda's room.

She was sitting up in bed making a drawing in black
crayon on to white cardboard, she was talking to him as he
was coming into the room, 'Why are you so out of breath?'
Henry sat on the bed, 'I ran up the stairs, I saw a man
asleep in one of the bedrooms, looked as though he was
dead.' Linda let the drawing fall to the floor, she laughed,
'That's Theo, didn't I tell you about him?' She pulled the
sheet up round her chin, 'I wake up early on Sunday but I

don't get up till it's lunch.' He showed her the clothes,
'Your mother gave me these, where can I get changed?'
'In here, of course, there's a hanger by your foot and you
can put your suit in the cupboard.' She pulled the sheet
up farther so that now just her eyes were visible, watching
him hang his suit up, come to sit down by her again without his trousers or jacket where he could feel against his
bare legs the warmth of her body through the thick rugs,
let his weight rest on her feet, stared at the yellow hair
spread on the pillow like a fan. They both laughed
suddenly at nothing, Linda slipped her hand out of the
bed, pulled at his elbow. 'Why don't you get inside too?'
Henry stood up, 'All right.' She ducked under the covers
giggling, calling out in a muffled way, 'But you have to
take all your clothes off first.' He did that, climbed in beside her, his body cooler than Linda's and making her
shiver when he lay down, his chest into her back. She
rolled over to face him, in the pink gloom she smelled
animal and milky, this was the beginning and end of his
Sunday when he came to recall it to himself, his heart
thumping from the pillow to his ear, lifting his head once
to let her free her hair, and talking, mostly about school,
her first week there, the friends they knew and the teachers,
it did not seem possible the day was taken with other
things, that he put on Linda's jeans and sweater, ate his
lunch and walked with the thousands milling without
direction on Hampstead Heath, and let Linda show him
the pictures in Kenwood House, cold superior ladies,
their unlikely children, and standing a long time in front
of the Rembrandt agreeing it was the best there and maybe the best in the world, though Linda did not like the
darkness around the figure, she wanted to see his room,
then they sat in Samuel Johnson's summerhouse, sure he
was a famous writer but of what and when? and back

across the Heath with the hundreds in the winter gloom, he came out of the blankets for air and she leaned her face against his chest then came out herself, lay there with their foreheads touching and dozed for half an hour, did it happen in the half hour he slept, all a kind of extended dream. The real thing was lying down for half an hour or more, that's how it seemed that night when he was in his own bed, at home.

It was not quite how he thought, things are never as you think they are going to be, not exactly, for on the day she forgot the red light bulbs and it was too late now because the shops were closed, and the recipe for punch was in an envelope, no time to look for it now, instead Mina bought a crate of bottles, mostly wine, she said, because nearly everybody likes wine, and two flagons of cider for those who did not. It was not a tape recorder, Henry had never seen one of those, it was the old record player borrowed from Mrs Simpson's son and the old records borrowed from Mrs Simpson. In anticipation, acting out the party in his mind, the house was bigger, the rooms were halls, the guests dwarfed by the height of the ceilings, music pounding at them from all sides, the disguises exotic, foreign princes, ghouls, sea captains and the like, and him with the mask. But now it was near the time for the first guest to arrive, the rooms were the same size as always, and why not, the music was from one corner, scratchy and dull, and here were the first guests, Henry opening the door to them in his thirty-shilling face with a startled look, here were the guests disguised as ordinary people, was it a disguise at all? had they read the card closely? He stood by the door holding it open, silent, as they streamed past him, nodded, seemed to think there was nothing special about his mask, just someone's little boy holding open the door, they

streamed in in twos and fours, laughing and talking with
restraint, poured their own drinks and laughed and talked
with less restraint, men in grey suits and black suits and
their hands deep in their pockets swaying towards and
away from their neighbour as they talked, the women with
grey hair piled up, fingering their glasses, they all looked
the same. Mina was upstairs planning to drift down, fuse
unnoticed and disguised with her guests, he looked about,
she could be here already, there was no woman here who
looked like her, or man. He wandered between the talking
groups, there was something about the men, something
about the women, the hips of one, the shoulders of the
others, a short man, bald and scented, his neck was too
thin for his shirt, the tie knot the size of his fist, he leaned
over Henry as he passed by looking for Mina, 'You must
be Henry,' his voice was thin and rasped, 'you must be, I
can tell by the look on your face.' He straightened out to
laugh, turning to see if any of the others had heard his
good joke, Henry waited, it was like this in the shop waiting on other people's jokes. The bald short man turned
back to him, wanted to reconcile him, in a lower voice,
'I knew it was you of course by your height, dear. Do
you know who I am?' Henry shook his head, watching the
man place his fingers on his pate, lift the skin between
forefinger and thumb to show not brain or bone but hair,
frizzy black hair in waves, which he covered back now
with the skin of his head, 'Can you guess now? No?'
He was pleased, obviously pleased, he bent lower to
whisper in Henry's ear, 'It's your Aunt Lucy,' and then
walked away. Lucy, one of those aunts not an aunt, a
friend of Mina's who came to coffee in the mornings and
wanted Henry in her small theatre company, always
wanted him to join and was not put off by his refusals,
Mina, jealous perhaps, did not want him to join, there

was no danger. But Mina, which of these wide-hipped men, which of these stout women was she? or was she still waiting for them all to drink more wine? He drank wine through his mask, remembering his last first time, his dress soaking in a bucket afterwards, where was it now? He pushed the wine quickly down his throat, avoiding the taste, the furriness on his teeth unmoved by his tongue, looking for Mina, waiting for Linda who was to come soon, undisguised, he told her there was no need because she was not known, she was a stranger and all strangers are in disguise. But was this a party, where they all stood around, talked, made jokes, moved from one group to another, no one listening to the record player which could not be heard above the voices, no one changed the record, was this how it was at parties? He changed the record himself, reached out for the record cover, a peeling remnant of shredded cardboard, when a hand took his wrist, an old hand, and looking up he saw an old man, a very old man, stooped over one shoulder, cocked round a hump bulging just slightly under his jacket and a scrub of beard about his face with the hairs far apart, and above his lips an oily patch where it did not grow at all, this man took his wrist, gripped it then let his hand fall, 'Wouldn't bother, no one can hear it anyway.' Henry faced the man, picked up for his defence his wine glass, 'Are you someone in disguise, is everyone in disguise?' The man pointed over his shoulder, he was not hurt, 'How do you get to disguise this?' 'It could be all part of it, I mean padding or something ...' Henry trailed away, lost his voice in the din, the man was turning his back to him and calling out, 'Feel it, go on you feel it and tell me if that's padding or not.' Like the wine these things can be done if done quickly, push it quickly down your stomach, he reached out and touched the man's back, withdrew his hand, and again when the

man said that was not enough to tell if it was padding or
not, this time he fingered the hump, Henry in his smiling
horror face, the hair in all directions, the coloured lips
drenched in wine, this small grinning monster fingered the
old man's hump at once hard and yielding, till the man
was satisfied and turned round, 'You can't hide a thing
like that,' and walked to the other side of the room,
standing there alone grinning at the people and drinking
from his glass. Henry filled his glass and drank from it too,
wandering between the circles of talkers, their voices rose
and fell about him, wailing organ stops that made him
dizzy, needed to lean by the table for support, waiting,
where was Mina, where was Linda? They were none of
them baffled by each other, these talkers and drinkers,
assuming they were in some disguise they knew who they
were, found it easy to talk, there was no question of being
able to do what you want, when you are not yourself you
are still someone, and someone has to take the blame,
blame, blame for what? Henry held the table tighter by
the edge with both hands, what blame? what was he
thinking just now? More wine more wine, something
nervous made him bring the glass to his mouth every ten
seconds, for not being noticed, for being no one at a grown-
ups' party, some small boy who held the door open when
they came in, for it not being crisp, as he had imagined it,
for all this he took in four glasses of wine. On the far side
of the room a man came away from a group, tottering
backwards with a glass in his hand, he fell into the large
chair behind him, and lay there laughing up at his friends
laughing down at him. Henry's words staggered on in his
head like big numbers on a board, occurring to him slowly,
if he left the table he would fall on the ground. Was it the
monster who fell to the ground or Henry, who was to
blame? it came back to him now, dressed like somebody

else and pretending to be them you took their blame for what they did, or what you as them do ... did? the big numbers were so slow, there was something in all this, when Mina dressed for dinner who did she think she was when she did what she did? The dress in the bucket like a rare sea animal, they stood in the deserted playground and made a joke about what you could do in disguise and Claire was walking towards them looking old and young, and the military officer who wiped his leg with a towel, the man in the bed, the black behind Rembrandt's head, Linda over there said she preferred, Linda over there, there was Linda on the other side of the room, her back to him, her waterfall of hair like Alice in Wonderland, there were too many other voices for her to hear him calling, he could not let go of the table. And she was talking to the man who fell in the chair, the man in the chair, the man in the chair, these big numbers, the man in the chair was pulling Linda on to his lap, Linda and Henry, he stood in front of his bedroom mirror feeling free, made a little dance as Henry and Linda, was pulling Linda on to his lap held her tight there behind her head, she was too frightened to move, terrified and could not make her tongue move and who would hear her in all these voices? was unbuttoning his shirt with one hand the man in the chair, the voices made a crescendo this dissonant choir, no one could see, the man in the chair pressed her face tight against him, would not let her go, Henry thought who was to blame? letting go of the table he began, but unsteadily and very slowly and the wine rising from his stomach, began to move towards them across the crowded room.

TALKING IT OVER
by Julian Barnes

Through the indelible voices of three narrators—two best friends and the woman they both love—Julian Barnes reconstructs the romantic triangle as a weapon whose edges cut like razor blades.

"An interplay of serious thought and dazzling wit.... It's moving, it's funny, it's frightening...fiction at its best."   —*The New York Times Book Review*

Fiction/Literature/0-679-73687-5/$11.00 (Can. $14.00)

POSSESSION
by A. S. Byatt

An intellectual mystery and a triumphant love story of a pair of young scholars researching the lives of two Victorian poets.

"Gorgeously written...dazzling...a tour de force."

—*The New York Times Book Review*

Fiction/Literature/0-679-73590-9/$12.00

THE STRANGER
by Albert Camus

Through the story of an ordinary man who unwittingly gets drawn into a senseless murder, Camus explores what he termed "the nakedness of man faced with the absurd."

Fiction/Literature/0-679-72020-0/$8.00

BREAKFAST AT TIFFANY'S
AND THREE STORIES
by Truman Capote

Truman Capote created in Holly Golightly a heroine whose name has entered the American idiom and whose style is now part of the literary landscape. Holly knows that nothing bad can ever happen to you at Tiffany's; her poignancy, wit, and naïveté continue to charm.

Also included in this volume are the stories "House of Flowers," "A Diamond Guitar," and "A Christmas Memory."

"Truman Capote is the most perfect writer of my generation. He writes the best sentences word for word, rhythm upon rhythm."   —Norman Mailer

Fiction/Literature/0-679-74565-3/$10.00 (Can. $13.00)

INVISIBLE MAN
by Ralph Ellison

This searing record of a black man's journey through contemporary America reveals, in Ralph Ellison's words, "the sheer rhetorical challenge involved in communicating across our barriers of race and religion, class, color and region."

"The greatest American novel in the second half of the twentieth century...the classic representation of American black experience."　　—R.W. B. Lewis

Fiction/Literature/0-679-72313-7/$10.00 (Can. $12.50)

....

THE SOUND AND THE FURY
by William Faulkner

The tragedy of the Compson family, featuring some of the most memorable characters in American literature: beautiful, rebellious Caddy; the manchild Benjy; haunted, neurotic Quentin; Jason, the brutal cynic; and Dilsey, their black servant.

"For range of effect, philosophical weight, originality of style, variety of characterization, humor, and tragic intensity, [Faulkner's works] are without equal in our time and country."　　—Robert Penn Warren

Fiction/Literature/0-679-73224-1/$9.00 (Can. $11.50)

....

A ROOM WITH A VIEW
by E. M. Forster

Caught up in a world of social snobbery, Lucy Honeychurch breaks from the claustrophobic constraints of her British guardians and takes control of her own fate, finding love with a man whose free spirit reminds her of a "room with a view."

Fiction/Literature/0-679-72476-1/$9.00 (Can. $11.50)

....

THE REMAINS OF THE DAY
by Kazuo Ishiguro

A profoundly compelling portrait of the perfect English butler and of his fading, insular world in postwar England.

"One of the best books of the year."　　—*The New York Times Book Review*

Fiction/Literature/0-679-73172-5/$11.00

....

THE WOMAN WARRIOR
by Maxine Hong Kingston

"A remarkable book...As an account of growing up female and Chinese-American in California, in a laundry of course, it is anti-nostalgic; it burns the fat right out of the mind. As a dream—of the 'female avenger'—it is dizzying, elemental, a poem turned into a sword."　　—*The New York Times*

Nonfiction/Literature/0-679-72188-6/$10.00 (Can. $12.50)

ALL THE PRETTY HORSES
by Cormac McCarthy

At sixteen, John Grady Cole finds himself at the end of a long line of Texas ranchers, cut off from the only life he has ever imagined for himself. With two companions, he sets off for Mexico on a sometimes idyllic, sometimes comic journey, to a place where dreams are paid for in blood.

"A book of remarkable beauty and strength, the work of a master in perfect command of his medium."   —*Washington Post Book World*

Winner of the National Book Award for Fiction
Fiction/Literature/0-679-74439-8/$12.00 (Can. $16.00)
....

DEATH IN VENICE
AND SEVEN OTHER STORIES
by Thomas Mann

In addition to "Death in Venice" ("A story," Mann said, "of death...of the voluptuousness of doom"), this volume includes "Mario the Magician," "Disorder and Early Sorrow," "A Man and His Dog," "Felix Krull," "The Blood of the Walsungs," "Tristan," and "Tonio Kröger."

Fiction/Literature/0-679-72206-8/$10.00 (Can. $12.50)
....

LOLITA
by Vladimir Nabokov

The famous and controversial novel that tells the story of the aging Humbert Humbert's obsessive, devouring, and doomed passion for the nymphet Dolores Haze.

"The only convincing love story of our century."   —*Vanity Fair*

Fiction/Literature/0-679-72316-1/$9.00 (Can. $11.50)
....

THE ENGLISH PATIENT
by Michael Ondaatje

During the final moments of World War II, four damaged people come together in a deserted Italian villa. As their stories unfold, a complex tapestry of image and emotion, recollection and observation is woven, leaving them inextricably connected by the brutal, improbable circumstances of war.

"It seduces and beguiles us with its many-layered mysteries, its brilliantly taut and lyrical prose, its tender regard for its characters."   —*Newsday*

Winner of the Booker Prize
Fiction/Literature/0-679-74520-3/$11.00
....

MATING
by Norman Rush

A female American anthropologist of high intellect and grand passion, at loose ends in Botswana, finds love with Nelson Denoon, a charismatic intellectual who is rumored to have founded a utopian society in the Kalahari Desert.

"A complex and moving love story...breathtaking in its cunningly intertwined intellectual sweep and brio...a major novel." —*Chicago Tribune*

Winner of the National Book Award for Fiction
Fiction/Literature/0-679-73709-X/$12.00 (Can. $15.00)

SOPHIE'S CHOICE
by William Styron

A young Southerner who yearns to become a writer befriends Nathan, a tortured, brilliant Jew, and his beautiful lover, Sophie, becoming a witness to their turbulent love-hate affair and to the burdens of Sophie's unbearable secret.

"Styron's most impressive performance.... It belongs on that small shelf reserved for American masterpieces." —*Washington Post Book World*

Fiction/Literature/0-679-73637-9/$13.00 (Can. $16.50)

WATERLAND
by Graham Swift

Set in the bleak Fen country of East Anglia and spanning some 240 years, *Waterland* is "a gothic family saga, a detective story and a philosophical meditation on the nature and uses of history" (*The New York Times*).

"Teems with energy, fertility, violence, madness...demonstrates the irrepressible, wide-ranging talent of this young British writer."

—*Washington Post Book World*

Fiction/Literature/0-679-73979-3/$11.00

THE PASSION
by Jeanette Winterson

Intertwining the destinies of two remarkable people—the soldier Henri, for eight years Napoleon's faithful cook, and Villanelle, the red-haired daughter of a Venetian boatman—*The Passion* is "a deeply imagined and beautiful book, often arrestingly so" (*The New York Times Book Review*).

Fiction/Literature/0-679-72437-0/$10.00

Available at your local bookstore, or call toll-free to order:
1-800-733-3000 (credit cards only). Prices subject to change.

VINTAGE INTERNATIONAL

____ **The Ark Sakura** by Kobo Abe $8.95   0-679-72161-4

____ **The Woman in the Dunes** by Kobo Abe $11.00   0-679-73378-7

____ **Chromos** by Felipe Alfau $11.00   0-679-73443-0

____ **Locos: A Comedy of Gestures** by Felipe Alfau $8.95   0-679-72846-5

____ **Dead Babies** by Martin Amis $10.00   0-679-73449-X

____ **Einstein's Monsters** by Martin Amis $8.95   0-679-72996-8

____ **London Fields** by Martin Amis $13.00   0-679-73034-6

____ **The Rachel Papers** by Martin Amis $10.00   0-679-73458-9

____ **Success** by Martin Amis $10.00   0-679-73448-1

____ **Time's Arrow** by Martin Amis $10.00   0-679-73572-0

____ **For Every Sin** by Aharon Appelfeld $9.95   0-679-72758-2

____ **One Day of Life** by Manlio Argueta $10.00   0-679-73243-8

____ **Collected Poems** by W. H. Auden $22.50   0-679-73197-0

____ **The Dyer's Hand** by W. H. Auden $15.00   0-679-72484-2

____ **Forewords and Afterwords** by W. H. Auden $15.00   0-679-72485-0

____ **Selected Poems** by W. H. Auden $11.00   0-679-72483-4

____ **Another Country** by James Baldwin $12.00   0-679-74471-1

____ **The Fire Next Time** by James Baldwin $8.00   0-679-74472-X

____ **Nobody Knows My Name** by James Baldwin $10.00   0-679-74473-8

____ **Doctor Copernicus** by John Banville $10.00   0-679-73799-5

____ **Kepler** by John Banville $10.00   0-679-74370-7

____ **Before She Met Me** by Julian Barnes $10.00   0-679-73609-3

____ **Flaubert's Parrot** by Julian Barnes $10.00   0-679-73136-9

____ **A History of the World in 10½ Chapters**
by Julian Barnes $12.00   0-679-73137-7

____ **Metroland** by Julian Barnes $10.00   0-679-73608-5

____ **The Porcupine** by Julian Barnes $9.00   0-679-74482-7

____ **Staring at the Sun** by Julian Barnes $10.00   0-679-74820-2

____ **Talking It Over** by Julian Barnes $11.00   0-679-73687-5

____ **The Italics Are Mine** by Nina Berberova $16.00   0-679-74537-8

____ **The Tattered Cloak and Other Novels**
by Nina Berberova $11.00   0-679-73366-3

____ **About Looking** by John Berger $10.00   0-679-73655-7

____ **And Our Faces, My Heart, Brief as Photos**
by John Berger $9.00   0-679-73656-5

____ **G.** by John Berger $11.00   0-679-73654-9

____ **Keeping a Rendezvous** by John Berger $12.00   0-679-73714-6

____ **Lilac and Flag** by John Berger $11.00   0-679-73719-7

____ **Once in Europa** by John Berger $11.00   0-679-73716-2

____ **Pig Earth** by John Berger $11.00   0-679-73715-4

____ **The Sense of Sight** by John Berger $12.00   0-679-73722-7

____ **The Success and Failure of Picasso**
by John Berger $12.00   0-679-73725-1

____ **Gathering Evidence** by Thomas Bernhard $14.00   0-679-73809-6

____ **The Loser** by Thomas Bernhard $10.00   0-679-74179-8

____ **A Man for All Seasons** by Robert Bolt $8.00   0-679-72822-8

VINTAGE INTERNATIONAL

___ The Sheltering Sky by Paul Bowles	$11.00	0-679-72979-8
___ An Act of Terror by André Brink	$14.00	0-679-74429-0
___ The Game by A.S. Byatt	$10.00	0-679-74256-5
___ Passions of the Mind by A.S. Byatt	$12.00	0-679-73678-6
___ Possession by A.S. Byatt	$12.00	0-679-73590-9
___ Sugar and Other Stories by A.S. Byatt	$10.00	0-679-74227-1
___ The Virgin in the Garden by A.S. Byatt	$12.00	0-679-73829-0
___ The Marriage of Cadmus and Harmony by Roberto Calasso	$13.00	0-679-73348-5
___ Six Memos for the Next Millennium by Italo Calvino	$10.00	0-679-74237-9
___ Exile and the Kingdom by Albert Camus	$10.00	0-679-73385-X
___ The Fall by Albert Camus	$9.00	0-679-72022-7
___ The Myth of Sisyphus and Other Essays by Albert Camus	$9.00	0-679-73373-6
___ The Plague by Albert Camus	$10.00	0-679-72021-9
___ The Rebel by Albert Camus	$11.00	0-679-73384-1
___ The Stranger by Albert Camus	$8.00	0-679-72020-0
___ Breakfast at Tiffany's by Truman Capote	$10.00	0-679-74565-3
___ The Grass Harp by Truman Capote	$10.00	0-679-74557-2
___ In Cold Blood by Truman Capote	$12.00	0-679-74558-0
___ Other Voices, Other Rooms by Truman Capote	$11.00	0-679-74564-5
___ The Fat Man in History by Peter Carey	$10.00	0-679-74332-4
___ The Tax Inspector by Peter Carey	$11.00	0-679-73598-4
___ Bullet Park by John Cheever	$10.00	0-679-73787-1
___ Falconer by John Cheever	$10.00	0-679-73786-3
___ Oh What a Paradise It Seems by John Cheever	$8.00	0-679-73785-5
___ The Wapshot Chronicle by John Cheever	$11.00	0-679-73899-1
___ The Wapshot Scandal by John Cheever	$11.00	0-679-73900-9
___ No Telephone to Heaven by Michelle Cliff	$11.00	0-679-73942-4
___ Age of Iron by J.M. Coetzee	$10.00	0-679-73292-6
___ After Henry by Joan Didion	$12.00	0-679-74539-4
___ Anecdotes of Destiny and Ehrengard by Isak Dinesen	$12.00	0-679-74333-2
___ Last Tales by Isak Dinesen	$13.00	0-679-73640-9
___ Out of Africa and Shadows on the Grass by Isak Dinesen	$12.00	0-679-72475-3
___ Seven Gothic Tales by Isak Dinesen	$12.00	0-679-73641-7
___ Winter's Tales by Isak Dinesen	$12.00	0-679-74334-0
___ The Book of Daniel by E.L. Doctorow	$10.00	0-679-73657-3
___ Loon Lake by E.L. Doctorow	$10.00	0-679-73625-5
___ Ragtime by E.L. Doctorow	$10.00	0-679-73626-3
___ Welcome to Hard Times by E.L. Doctorow	$10.00	0-679-73627-1
___ World's Fair by E.L. Doctorow	$11.00	0-679-73628-X
___ Love, Pain, and the Whole Damn Thing by Doris Dörrie	$9.00	0-679-72992-5

VINTAGE INTERNATIONAL

___ The **Assignment** by Friedrich Dürrenmatt	$7.95	0-679-72233-5
___ **Invisible Man** by Ralph Ellison	$10.00	0-679-72313-7
___ **Scandal** by Shusaku Endo	$10.00	0-679-72355-2
___ **Absalom, Absalom!** by William Faulkner	$9.95	0-679-73218-7
___ **As I Lay Dying** by William Faulkner	$9.00	0-679-73225-X
___ **Go Down, Moses** by William Faulkner	$10.00	0-679-73217-9
___ **The Hamlet** by William Faulkner	$10.00	0-679-73653-0
___ **Intruder in the Dust** by William Faulkner	$9.00	0-679-73651-4
___ **Light in August** by William Faulkner	$10.00	0-679-73226-8
___ **The Reivers** by William Faulkner	$10.00	0-679-74192-5
___ **Sanctuary** by William Faulkner	$10.00	0-679-74814-8
___ **The Sound and the Fury** by William Faulkner	$9.00	0-679-73224-1
___ **The Unvanquished** by William Faulkner	$9.00	0-679-73652-2
___ **The Good Soldier** by Ford Madox Ford	$10.00	0-679-72218-1
___ **Howards End** by E. M. Forster	$10.00	0-679-72255-6
___ **The Longest Journey** by E. M. Forster	$11.00	0-679-74815-6
___ **A Room With a View** by E. M. Forster	$9.00	0-679-72476-1
___ **Where Angels Fear to Tread** by E. M. Forster	$9.00	0-679-73634-4
___ **Christopher Unborn** by Carlos Fuentes	$14.00	0-679-73222-5
___ **The Story of My Wife** by Milán Füst	$8.95	0-679-72217-3
___ **The Story of a Shipwrecked Sailor** by Gabriel García Márquez	$9.00	0-679-72205-X
___ **The Tin Drum** by Günter Grass	$15.00	0-679-72575-X
___ **Claudius the God** by Robert Graves	$14.00	0-679-72573-3
___ **I, Claudius** by Robert Graves	$12.00	0-679-72477-X
___ **Dispatches** by Michael Herr	$10.00	0-679-73525-9
___ **Walter Winchell** by Michael Herr	$9.00	0-679-73393-0
___ **The Swimming-Pool Library** by Alan Hollinghurst	$12.00	0-679-72256-4
___ **I Served the King of England** by Bohumil Hrabal	$12.00	0-679-72786-8
___ **An Artist of the Floating World** by Kazuo Ishiguro	$10.00	0-679-72266-1
___ **A Pale View of Hills** by Kazuo Ishiguro	$10.00	0-679-72267-X
___ **The Remains of the Day** by Kazuo Ishiguro	$11.00	0-679-73172-5
___ **A Neil Jordan Reader** by Neil Jordan	$12.00	0-679-74834-2
___ **Dubliners** by James Joyce	$10.00	0-679-73990-4
___ **A Portrait of the Artist as a Young Man** by James Joyce	$9.00	0-679-73989-0
___ **Ulysses** by James Joyce	$15.00	0-679-72276-9
___ **The Emperor** by Ryszard Kapuściński	$9.00	0-679-72203-3
___ **Shah of Shahs** by Ryszard Kapuściński	$10.00	0-679-73801-0
___ **The Soccer War** by Ryszard Kapuściński	$10.00	0-679-73805-3
___ **China Men** by Maxine Hong Kingston	$10.00	0-679-72328-5
___ **Tripmaster Monkey** by Maxine Hong Kingston	$11.00	0-679-72789-2
___ **The Woman Warrior** by Maxine Hong Kingston	$10.00	0-679-72188-6

VINTAGE INTERNATIONAL

____ **Love and Garbage** by Ivan Klíma	$11.00	0-679-73755-3
____ **Barabbas** by Pär Lagerkvist	$8.00	0-679-72544-X
____ **The Plumed Serpent** by D. H. Lawrence	$12.00	0-679-73493-7
____ **The Virgin & the Gipsy** by D. H. Lawrence	$10.00	0-679-74077-5
____ **The Radiance of the King** by Camara Laye	$12.00	0-679-72200-9
____ **Canopus in Argos** by Doris Lessing	$20.00	0-679-74184-4
____ **The Fifth Child** by Doris Lessing	$9.00	0-679-72182-7
____ **The Drowned and the Saved** by Primo Levi	$10.00	0-679-72186-X
____ **My Traitor's Heart** by Rian Malan	$10.95	0-679-73215-2
____ **The Great World** by David Malouf	$12.00	0-679-74836-9
____ **Man's Fate** by André Malraux	$11.00	0-679-72574-1
____ **Buddenbrooks** by Thomas Mann	$14.00	0-679-73646-8
____ **Confessions of Felix Krull** by Thomas Mann	$11.00	0-679-73904-1
____ **Death in Venice and Seven Other Stories** by Thomas Mann	$10.00	0-679-72206-8
____ **Doctor Faustus** by Thomas Mann	$13.00	0-679-73905-X
____ **The Magic Mountain** by Thomas Mann	$14.00	0-679-73645-X
____ **All the Pretty Horses** by Cormac McCarthy	$12.00	0-679-74439-8
____ **Blood Meridian** by Cormac McCarthy	$11.00	0-679-72875-9
____ **Child of God** by Cormac McCarthy	$10.00	0-679-72874-0
____ **Outer Dark** by Cormac McCarthy	$10.00	0-679-72873-2
____ **Suttree** by Cormac McCarthy	$12.00	0-679-73632-8
____ **The Cement Garden** by Ian McEwan	$10.00	0-679-75018-5
____ **First Love, Last Rites** by Ian McEwan	$10.00	0-679-75019-3
____ **The Captive Mind** by Czeslaw Milosz	$10.00	0-679-72856-2
____ **The Decay of the Angel** by Yukio Mishima	$12.00	0-679-72243-2
____ **Runaway Horses** by Yukio Mishima	$13.00	0-679-72240-8
____ **Spring Snow** by Yukio Mishima	$12.00	0-679-72241-6
____ **The Temple of Dawn** by Yukio Mishima	$12.00	0-679-72242-4
____ **Such a Long Journey** by Rohinton Mistry	$11.00	0-679-73871-1
____ **Hopeful Monsters** by Nicholas Mosley	$13.00	0-679-73929-7
____ **Cities of Salt** by Abdelrahman Munif	$16.00	0-394-75526-X
____ **The Trench** by Abdelrahman Munif	$14.00	0-679-74533-5
____ **Hard-Boiled Wonderland and the End of the World** by Haruki Murakami	$12.00	0-679-74346-4
____ **The Spyglass Tree** by Albert Murray	$10.00	0-679-73085-0
____ **Ada, or Ardor** by Vladimir Nabokov	$15.00	0-679-72522-9
____ **Bend Sinister** by Vladimir Nabokov	$11.00	0-679-72727-2
____ **The Defense** by Vladimir Nabokov	$11.00	0-679-72722-1
____ **Despair** by Vladimir Nabokov	$11.00	0-679-72343-9
____ **The Enchanter** by Vladimir Nabokov	$10.00	0-679-72886-4
____ **The Eye** by Vladimir Nabokov	$8.95	0-679-72723-X
____ **The Gift** by Vladimir Nabokov	$11.00	0-679-72725-6
____ **Glory** by Vladimir Nabokov	$10.00	0-679-72724-8
____ **Invitation to a Beheading** by Vladimir Nabokov	$9.00	0-679-72531-8
____ **King, Queen, Knave** by Vladimir Nabokov	$11.00	0-679-72340-4

___ **Laughter in the Dark** by Vladimir Nabokov $11.00   0-679-72450-8

___ **Lolita** by Vladimir Nabokov $9.00   0-679-72316-1

___ **Look at the Harlequins!** by Vladimir Nabokov $9.95   0-679-72728-0

___ **Mary** by Vladimir Nabokov $10.00   0-679-72620-9

___ **Pale Fire** by Vladimir Nabokov $11.00   0-679-72342-0

___ **Pnin** by Vladimir Nabokov $10.00   0-679-72341-2

___ **The Real Life of Sebastian Knight** $10.00   0-679-72726-4
     by Vladimir Nabokov

___ **Speak, Memory** by Vladimir Nabokov $12.00   0-679-72339-0

___ **Strong Opinions** by Vladimir Nabokov $12.00   0-679-72609-8

___ **Transparent Things** by Vladimir Nabokov $6.95   0-679-72541-5

___ **A Bend in the River** by V. S. Naipaul $10.00   0-679-72202-5

___ **Guerrillas** by V. S. Naipaul $10.95   0-679-73174-1

___ **A Turn in the South** by V. S. Naipaul $11.00   0-679-72488-5

___ **The English Patient** by Michael Ondaatje $11.00   0-679-74520-3

___ **Running in the Family** by Michael Ondaatje $10.00   0-679-74669-2

___ **Body Snatcher** by Juan Carlos Onetti $13.00   0-679-73887-8

___ **Black Box** by Amos Oz $10.00   0-679-72185-1

___ **My Michael** by Amos Oz $11.00   0-679-72804-X

___ **The Slopes of Lebanon** by Amos Oz $11.00   0-679-73144-X

___ **Metaphor and Memory** by Cynthia Ozick $13.00   0-679-73425-2

___ **The Shawl** by Cynthia Ozick $7.95   0-679-72926-7

___ **Dictionary of the Khazars** by Milorad Pavić
     male edition $9.95   0-679-72461-3
     female edition $9.95   0-679-72754-X

___ **Landscape Painted with Tea** by Milorad Pavić $12.00   0-679-73344-2

___ **Truck Stop Rainbows** by Iva Pekárková $11.00   0-679-74675-7

___ **Cambridge** by Caryl Phillips $10.00   0-679-73689-1

___ **Complete Collected Stories** by V. S. Pritchett $20.00   0-679-73892-4

___ **Swann's Way** by Marcel Proust $13.00   0-679-72009-X

___ **Kiss of the Spider Woman** by Manuel Puig $11.00   0-679-72449-4

___ **Grey Is the Color of Hope** by Irina Ratushinskaya $8.95   0-679-72447-8

___ **Memoirs of an Anti-Semite** $12.00   0-679-73182-2
     by Gregor von Rezzori

___ **The Orient-Express** by Gregor von Rezzori $11.00   0-679-74822-9

___ **The Snows of Yesteryear** by Gregor von Rezzori $10.95   0-679-73181-4

___ **The Notebooks of Malte Laurids Brigge** $12.00   0-679-73245-4
     by Rainer Maria Rilke

___ **Selected Poetry** by Rainer Maria Rilke $12.00   0-679-72201-7

___ **Goodbye, Columbus** by Philip Roth $11.00   0-679-74826-1

___ **My Life as a Man** by Philip Roth $11.00   0-679-74827-X

___ **Mating** by Norman Rush $12.00   0-679-73709-X

___ **Whites** by Norman Rush $9.00   0-679-73816-9

___ **The Age of Reason** by Jean-Paul Sartre $12.00   0-679-73895-9

___ **No Exit and 3 Other Plays** by Jean-Paul Sartre $10.00   0-679-72516-4

___ **The Reprieve** by Jean-Paul Sartre $12.00   0-679-74078-3

VINTAGE INTERNATIONAL

___ Troubled Sleep by Jean-Paul Sartre	$12.00	0-679-74079-1
___ Open Doors and Three Novellas	$12.00	0-679-73561-5
by Leonardo Sciascia		
___ All You Who Sleep Tonight by Vikram Seth	$7.00	0-679-73025-7
___ The Golden Gate by Vikram Seth	$12.00	0-679-73457-0
___ And Quiet Flows the Don by Mikhail Sholokhov	$15.00	0-679-72521-0
___ By Grand Central Station I Sat Down and Wept	$10.00	0-679-73804-5
by Elizabeth Smart		
___ Ake: The Years of Childhood by Wole Soyinka	$11.00	0-679-72540-7
___ Ìsarà: A Voyage Around "Essay"	$9.95	0-679-73246-2
by Wole Soyinka		
___ Children of Light by Robert Stone	$10.00	0-679-73593-3
___ A Flag for Sunrise by Robert Stone	$12.00	0-679-73762-6
___ Confessions of Nat Turner by William Styron	$12.00	0-679-73663-8
___ Lie Down in Darkness by William Styron	$12.00	0-679-73597-6
___ The Long March and In the Clap Shack	$11.00	0-679-73675-1
by William Styron		
___ Set This House on Fire by William Styron	$12.00	0-679-73674-3
___ Sophie's Choice by William Styron	$13.00	0-679-73637-9
___ This Quiet Dust by William Styron	$12.00	0-679-73596-8
___ Confessions of Zeno by Italo Svevo	$12.00	0-679-72234-3
___ Ever After by Graham Swift	$11.00	0-679-74026-0
___ Learning to Swim by Graham Swift	$9.00	0-679-73978-5
___ Out of This World by Graham Swift	$10.00	0-679-74032-5
___ Shuttlecock by Graham Swift	$10.00	0-679-73933-5
___ The Sweet-Shop Owner by Graham Swift	$10.00	0-679-73980-7
___ Waterland by Graham Swift	$11.00	0-679-73979-3
___ The Beautiful Mrs. Seidenman	$9.95	0-679-73214-4
by Andrzej Szczypiorski		
___ Diary of a Mad Old Man by Junichiro Tanizaki	$10.00	0-679-73024-9
___ The Key by Junichiro Tanizaki	$10.00	0-679-73023-0
___ On the Golden Porch by Tatyana Tolstaya	$11.00	0-679-72843-0
___ Sleepwalker in a Fog by Tatyana Tolstaya	$10.00	0-679-73063-X
___ The Real Life of Alejandro Mayta	$12.00	0-679-72478-8
by Mario Vargas Llosa		
___ The Eye of the Story by Eudora Welty	$8.95	0-679-73004-4
___ Losing Battles by Eudora Welty	$11.00	0-679-72882-1
___ The Optimist's Daughter by Eudora Welty	$9.00	0-679-72883-X
___ The Passion by Jeanette Winterson	$10.00	0-679-72437-0
___ Sexing the Cherry by Jeanette Winterson	$10.00	0-679-73316-7
___ Written on the Body by Jeanette Winterson	$11.00	0-679-74447-9

Available at your bookstore or call toll-free to order: 1-800-733-3000.
Credit cards only. Prices subject to change.